COLDHEARTED BASTARD

UNDERWORLD KINGS

JENIKA SNOW

COLDHEARTED BASTARD (Underworld Kings)

By Jenika Snow

www.JenikaSnow.com

Jenika_Snow@Yahoo.com

Copyright © October 2021 by Jenika Snow

First E-book Publication: October 2021

Photographer and image provided by: Shuttersock

Cover design by: Cormar Covers

Editors: Kayla Robichaux, Lea Ann Schafer

Beta Reader: Judy Ann Loves Books

COLD
HEARTED
Bastard

USA Today Bestselling Author
JENIKA SNOW

He didn't have a heart... but he wanted hers.

All I knew about life was anger and violence. Pain and suffering. Kill or be killed.

I was a "fixer" for the Ruin—a syndicate for the Bratva, Cosa Nostra, Cartel, and any other organized crime faction that dealt in the darker, crueler aspects of humanity.

I was a free agent who was called upon to do things weaker men didn't have the stomach for.

And when you surround yourself with death for long enough, soon you don't remember what it felt like to be alive.

And then I saw her. She was a fragile little thing who tried to be strong. But I could tell she'd seen too much horror in the world, too much of the ugly within people. I should have stayed away. I'd only bring her further down into the darkness.

But for the first time in my life, I felt a stirring in my chest, this protectiveness and possessiveness toward another living person. And it was painful. It made me feel alive.

Lina tried to hide how broken she was, but I was an old friend of being ruined. She held secrets I'd find out. Because for the first time in my miserable life, I wanted something for myself. I felt something more than apathy and indifference.

I wanted to possess the innocence she clung to. I wanted to break it open and consume it for myself.

I could look into her too trusting blue eyes and knew I'd maim for her. I'd kill for her. And that became our truth when her past finally came back for her, when my present tried to destroy her.

They thought they could take the one thing—the *only* thing—I'd ever wanted for myself. They were wrong.

When I looked at her, I felt some of the monster that made me who I was retreat back to my black soul. He'd never leave... but he'd share the space.

For her.

1

Galina

Two months ago

I was pushed from behind so hard I lost my balance and fell forward, my hands instinctively reaching out to stop the impact. My knees and palms connected with the dirty ground, tearing at skin, pain lancing up my arms and legs.

I'd been brought to an abandoned warehouse. This could very well be where I died.

I heard snickering from the two men behind me, the ones who'd forcefully taken me out of my bed. I clenched my jaw, the familiar anger I felt whenever I thought of my father and the shit he dragged me into moving through me.

I was here because of *him*. My father. The lowlife drug addict who had a gambling problem and made a bet he couldn't talk his way out of. And he'd finally included me personally in his hellhole.

I should have left Vegas long ago, I thought. *I should have never convinced myself that I was stronger than all this shit, that I didn't have to leave to make a life for myself. Damn it, I should have put him and everything he stood for behind me for good.*

Would've, could've, should've, and all that bullshit.

For a second I contemplated just staying on my hands and knees. I wasn't sure if I was going to get kicked back down if I tried to rise, but I didn't want to seem weak. I refused to let these assholes think I was easy prey.

I gathered my pride and pushed myself up, the sound of the men in the room laughing causing me to grit my teeth and ignore them.

Because it was the middle of the night, I wore nothing but a white tank top and a pair of loose lounge pants. They hadn't even given me time to put on shoes or a jacket, and with it being October— even though we were in Vegas—the temperature dropped below fifty. Coupled with this dank, old warehouse and the fear that I'd probably die tonight —or worse—I started shivering.

I wrapped my arms around myself, wanting to conserve heat, and also because I could feel how hard my nipples were and didn't want the sick fucks getting a boner at the sight. I didn't look behind me at the two men who still stood there, blocking the entrance.

There were a handful of men standing in front of me, and I was surprised they needed so many bodies just for me. The warehouse I had been taken to was clearly abandoned, the floors filthy, age and rust covering every inch of this place. The scent of dirt, mold, and something rotting filled the air.

Given the fact that I was surrounded by a bunch of lowlifes, the smell of what was rotting could've very well been a body for all I knew.

I heard some shuffling to my side and turned my head to see my father stepping out from a doorway.

My father. The man I'd written off more than a year ago, pushed him out of my life because I was tired of him constantly pulling me into the vortex of his shit.

The steel door hung from rusted-out hinges and leaned half against the wall as he cleared the entry-way. At first I was confused why he didn't have anyone dragging his sorry ass forward. Was he here of his own free will? Seemed unlikely, given his track record.

But then I saw the barrel of a gun that was pointed right behind his head.

The man who stepped out from behind my father was tall and heavily muscled, his face expressionless.

When my father and the gunman cleared the doorway, I spotted another man stepping through. The master to these fucking puppets.

Henry Taedoni.

He was the only one I was familiar with in this shithole, but then again, that was only because of my father and all the trouble he constantly brought down in all our lives.

Henry was what many people in our circle would've called a gangster, although "many people in our circle" consisted of meth heads, gambling addicts, and anyone who owed him money. Henry was nothing more than a low-level loan shark, a drug dealer, and an all-around piece of shit.

He wasn't part of any official organized crime faction. I would've placed them in the white trash category, the kind of "leader" who kept addicts, criminals, and degenerates of the trashier variety on his payroll and as his clientele.

Because they were easily manipulated and wouldn't fight back.

Henry and his people weren't organized or smart. They used sloppy force and fear tactics toward an already weak population to get what they wanted.

"Galina Michone," he drawled in a way that made my skin prickle with awareness and disgust. He came closer and stopped when he was a few feet from me. A nasty grin spread across his face, a gold tooth in the side of his mouth flashing under the dirty, muted light. The way he let his gaze move up and down my body made me feel slimy and naked.

"Leo's really gotten himself into a jam this time," Henry murmured and tucked his hands into the front pockets of his slacks, ones that looked like they were made of discount polyester.

For all the money Henry had swindled out of people, he looked as cheap as a two-dollar bill.

"I'm not sure what Leo does or doesn't do has to do with me." I should've kept my mouth shut. Pissing off Leo and his goons wasn't going to do me any favors.

But I was surprised—and proud—I sounded as

strong as I did. Inside I was terrified, of course. I knew the situation wasn't going to go in my favor.

"Leo and I don't speak. He denounced me as his daughter quite a while ago when I refused to give him money and told him what a lowlife he was."

Henry grinned again, this one more sharklike.

"And even if I did have the money, which I don't, I sure as hell wouldn't use it to bail Leo out. He's on his own." I didn't bother looking at the man who'd been nothing but a sperm donor. Fuck him for getting me into this shit.

I looked back at Henry quickly, knowing I couldn't trust him as far as I could throw him. I noticed how he looked over my shoulder at the two men behind me, something in his eyes causing them to move closer. I heard the shuffling of their feet, smelled the dirty sweat that clung to them as it filled my nose. I tensed, my muscles tightening. Although I'd taken a few self-defense classes in the past, I wasn't a fool thinking I was any match for them.

"It's not money I want from you, Galina."

My heart stopped, then started racing over time.

"Leo finally offered compensation for his debt that I am satisfied with." Henry's grin couldn't be called anything but perverse. "And that's you—or more so your body and that sweet cherry you still have between your legs."

I felt my eyes widen a second before pure horror washed through me. I looked over at Leo, but the bastard wasn't looking at me, wouldn't dare face me after the heinous act he'd just done.

"And don't try saying you're not as innocent as Leo said. I've been watching you, Galina. I know you don't take company with anyone. I know your daily habits, know you sleep alone every night." Henry raked his beady-eyed gaze up and down my body and took a step toward me. "In fact, I've stood over your bed and watched you sleep, know you keep a pistol under your pillow." He hummed as if that aroused him. "I even leaned down and smelled your hair on more than one occasion, wondering if your pussy smells just as sweet."

Oh God. I took a step back, fear coursing through me, but my back slammed into one of his goons. Hands clamped around my arms, and I fought wildly, self-preservation rising up. I kicked and screamed, but it was only met with a bruising grip and laughter surrounding me. Soon enough, I was winded and defeated, tears springing to my eyes... ones I refused to let fall.

I didn't confirm or deny what Henry said. I

wouldn't give him the satisfaction of breaking down. I looked at Leo once more. He was staring at me with what I could have assumed was guilt, but he also looked high as a kite.

"You were supposed to protect me," I whispered. Those words were nothing but a pipe dream of a once vulnerable little girl. I had no mother, no father despite him standing right in front of me.

And he'd sold off my virginity to clear his debt. He sold me off as if I was a commodity.

"I think I'll let some fucker buy your cherry for an exorbitant price. You don't see many women still so innocent at your age."

Like my age of twenty-one meant I was some spinster.

"And after you've been broken in—defiled, I'm sure—then I'll take you for a ride before you really get used up." I snapped my focus back to Henry. "But you look so sweet and delicious that I may not tire of you for some time. I may keep you as my personal pet for a while, Galina." He was leering again like a sick fuck.

"And then what?" I sneered. Fuck him. Let him see my anger and wrath, even if it didn't do any good.

His grin widened. I was pretty sure he liked me fighting back, probably got off on it. "And then I'll sell you off nightly, recoup my money and then some."

I struggled all over again, managing to kick the leg of the bastard holding me. He grunted and dug his fingers into me so hard I knew there would be black-and-blue marks on my flesh. I hissed in pain, and he jerked me closer to him, my back to his chest, before he wrapped a steely arm around my middle, stilling me.

"If you don't stop, I'll knock you out with a hit to the face," he seethed, and I froze. His breath smelled like stale cigarette smoke and cheap liquor.

"Brutus, let's not resort to scare tactics." Henry clucked and moved closer until he stood right in front of me. He stared at me, the leering and suggestive looks suddenly gone as he became serious.

And that terrified me the most out of this entire situation.

"It could have been worse, Galina. So much worse."

I bit my tongue so I didn't say something I couldn't take back. I was still trying to think of how to get out of this, even if that seemed impossible.

"And hey," he said and grinned once more, holding his hands out as if he was some kind of martyr. "I'm not such a bad guy. I'm even going to let you go back home and gather anything you want that'll fit into a bag. I do want you to be comfortable... until you're not." He gave me a wink, and my belly clenched in dread.

I didn't ask why he was giving me that small "gift," because it allowed me more time to think of how to escape, of how to run. What Leo and Henry didn't know—what no one knew—was I had always felt like something bad was going to happen. That other shoe dropping. The end of the world... *my* world. And it was because of that that I'd already packed a bag, had escape money, no actual plan but a means to leave at the drop of a hat. If I could just get to where I'd stashed my bag and supplies, I had a chance. It was slim, but it was still a chance.

So I went slack in the asshole's arms until he loosened his hold on me enough I could breathe comfortably. Henry cocked his head, maybe thinking I was being a little too accepting of my situation, but I didn't care. I had to be smart if I wanted a chance to survive.

I gave my piece-of-shit father one last hateful look, swearing that if I ever had the chance, I'd end him, wipe out his miserable life like he'd so easily done with mine. I was then hauled away, pulled through the dirty warehouse, and tossed into the back of the car I'd been brought here in.

The next twenty minutes as we drove through Vegas and back to my crappy apartment went by in a blur. I didn't question why they hadn't just grabbed my stuff when they'd taken me from my apartment. I didn't wonder why they were even giving me this small "act of kindness". I didn't ask or care because in the end they didn't care. Hell, for all I knew this was all an act to make me more compliant, to make it seem like things weren't as bad as they were.

In the end my feelings and wants and needs, my comforts didn't matter.

I couldn't think straight, was sweaty and shaking, and I felt the glaring looks of the two men who sat on either side of me.

Before I knew it, I was hauled out of the back of the car and taken up to my apartment. Because my place was as shitty as they came, anyone we passed —even at this hour—minded their own business. They were either addicts and not coherent enough to care, or they knew who the men trailing me worked for and were too afraid to intervene.

"Grab your shit," one of the men said harshly as he pushed me into my apartment after the door was opened. It was shut behind me, and I started making my way toward my room, when I felt a tight grip on my forearm stop me.

"If you do anything stupid, I'll fucking beat you and say to hell with grabbing your shit. Got it?"

I didn't look at the prick who spoke the words, just nodded and tugged my arm free. "I have to use the bathroom."

"Make it quick." His words were clipped as he followed close behind me.

Before I could go inside, he pushed his way in front and surveyed the bathroom. It was tiny and old, with rust and calcium deposits and stains on the tub and sink, a small window above the tub. He went over to the window and tried opening it, and I held my breath, praying it held. It was old and janky, but I'd rigged it a certain way that I could open it where others would see it as sealed shut.

And when it held strong, he moved away, and I exhaled. He checked under the sink, presumably for weapons, but all he'd find was a couple of cleaning supplies, which he removed. What did he think I was going to do with them?

"Make it quick," he said again and left me alone, and I was shocked he allowed me to close the door. I wanted to thank whoever was listening, but I didn't have time. No one would help me but myself.

I opened the door under the sink, and as silently as I could, I popped up the loose wooden board where my bag was held. Once I had it, I grabbed the cheap sneakers inside, threw on a long-sleeved shirt, and made sure the money and gun were still tucked away. And then I went over to the toilet and flushed it, then quickly went to the window to pry it open. I hoped the flushed toilet would mask the sound of me opening the glass.

Once it was pried open, I tossed my bag out, my apartment fortunately close enough to the ground that I wouldn't break a leg jumping out.

I was halfway out when one of the assholes pounded on the door and barked out, "Hurry it the fuck up." And just as I swung my body out the window, I saw the bathroom door open and the prick barrel inside. His gaze latched on to me instantly, his eyes narrowing and a curse ringing out.

I landed on the ground and grabbed my bag, then ran like my life depended on it.

Because it did.

2

Arlo
Present day

My mother had been called a whore.

My father had been a *boyevik*—a soldier—for the Bratva.

I was an orphan at the age of eleven. A criminal at the age of twelve.

I was a murderer when I turned sixteen.

And here I was, fifteen years later, a coldhearted bastard.

You could have summed up my life in those details. The particulars didn't matter. The people I'd come in contact with were inconsequential. It was easy to pretend to have interest. It was effortless to act like I had a heart.

I'd been told a lot of things during my life, lies to make me fall in line.

"Your mother was nothing but a cheap slut. Women like that don't last long. They're used up and thrown away. They serve their purpose that way."

That had been one of the longest, most "heart-felt"—in my father's eyes—conversations he'd ever had with me. The truth, I'd later learn, had been far from what he told me.

I'd been taken from my mother's arms shortly after she'd been forced to give birth to me, thrown into the home of strangers associated with the Bratva—the Russian mafia. From the moment I drew my first breath, I'd been indoctrinated to the life of a criminal. Of death and hatred and loyalty to only one entity.

My mother had been a young Russian girl who had hopes and dreams. That was the fantasy I made up. That was the fantasy she was no doubt told to stay pliant and submissive. Hope could make anyone do whatever you wanted.

I didn't know her, didn't know anything about her from personal experience. She'd been taken from her bed in the middle of the night, trafficked to

America, and sold off like a piece of meat to those who had power and money.

Those I worked for. And sometimes those I killed.

Those who liked breaking things. Ruining them.

Those men who destroyed a person until there was nothing left but the darkness, that once hope now nothing but hopeless resignation.

The familiar anger I felt at thinking of the fate of my mother was like acid in my veins. I didn't let emotions play a factor in my life. They never had except for the thought of a mother I'd never known, a girl far too young, who'd been raped and beaten countless times, forced to push out a baby she probably didn't want, then used all over again.

She'd been the only thing I'd ever let my apathy go for. And a part of me hated that, hated her for making me feel anything other than the nothingness I was so very familiar with. The bleak darkness I embraced.

I didn't have to know her love to know she'd been innocent—like so many other young girls thrown into this life.

For a second I stared at my hands, ones that had been covered in blood many times over my thirty-one years. Hands that would soon be drenched in the life force of another.

They were fingers and palms that had killed mercilessly. Ones that had taken my father's life once I found out he'd been the one who raped my mother, fathered me, and ultimately killed her.

I didn't have to know the woman who birthed me to exact vengeance in her honor. It would never right the wrongs committed against her—or against any of the other helpless victims—but it sure as fuck made me feel better.

Patricide. Who knew it was what I'd been born to do? Who knew it was my own personal therapy?

And it was the act of killing my father that elevated me to the position I was in now with the Ruin and the Bratva. Apparently the Bratva thought I'd done them a favor by taking out my father—a traitor who'd been giving information to the Cosa Nostra.

I never corrected them, never told them that what I'd done, I'd done for myself and Sasha, that girl who'd been nothing but a child and had only been given hell on earth. Let the Bratva think I did what I did for them. It made no difference to the end result.

"I heard all the poor fucker did was look at the Pakhan's daughter, and it earned him *that* shit."

Just hearing about the Pakhan—Leonid Petrov, leader of the East Coast Bratva—had my skin tightening. I didn't respond or acknowledge what Maksim said. I glanced at him and watched as he pointed at the SOB who was about to be dismembered and dissolved. Maksim cursed in Russian, but I ignored him and focused on the job.

There was the sound of a lighter flaring, followed by the sweet, smoky scent of the cigarillos Maksim got from a connection he had with the Cartel. I'd learned that all in the span of the first five minutes of being in his presence tonight.

I was called, and I came. I did my job, got rid of the bodies, and went about my miserable fucking life.

"A damn *look*, Arlo," Maksim muttered under his breath, and I heard him take another drag. "Can you imagine—"

"No, because I don't fucking care about the circumstances." I cut him a glare. "A job is a job when the Ruin calls me." I tipped my chin toward the black barrel off to the side. "They let you come and learn something, so shut the fuck up and listen. Stop talking." I held his gaze with mine. "My job is to be effective and fast. Stop gossiping and get the fucking barrel."

Normally I did my job alone. It was easier. Quiet. I didn't want to fucking talk about the weather, let alone how one of these assholes kicked the bucket. I did what I was tasked to do, then put it behind me.

Because that's what you had to do when you were a fixer for the Ruin.

But Maksim was still young and dumb, without much experience, and certainly not where the Ruin or the Bratva were concerned. But because he was a blood relation to one of the higher-ups with the Russian mafia, they allowed him to worm his way into situations that should have been reserved for more controlled, skilled men.

And this was one of those situations. But pissing off someone higher up in the Bratva or Ruin food chain wasn't my style, or smart for that matter, so I kept my mouth shut and let the little shit learn a thing or two.

Because being a free agent for the syndicate known as the Ruin, one that dealt in everything illegal and underground, meant if you wanted to keep your balls, you didn't question shit.

When the Ruin called, I took the job and did it fucking well. I didn't care if it was for the Cosa

Nostra, the Bratva, or the fucking Cartel. I didn't give a shit who the job was for, as long as I got paid.

So as I looked at the bashed-in face of the body I was about to dispose of, all I saw was a means to an end.

"I heard they took a melon baller to his fucking eyes."

I exhaled and felt my muscles tighten in annoyance. "For fuck's sake, Maksim," I said with unrestrained anger and cut a withering glare his way. He held up his hands and placed the thin brown cigarillo between his lips.

"I'm shutting up now," he murmured swiftly and walked over to the corner of the warehouse where the fifty-five-gallon barrel drum was stashed. I crouched and opened the large duffel bag, rifling through the supplies I'd need for this particular job.

Maksim brought over the two most important implements I'd need and set them beside me.

Butcher saw.

Lye.

The latter I'd brought over in abundance earlier.

Maksim dragged the barrel over to the body currently laid out on the plastic tarp. "They really did his face dirty—"

"*Maksim*," I growled and cut a glance his way. I

didn't need to say anything else for him to shut his trap and give a sharp nod. "Put that out."

He took the cigarillo from between his lips and snubbed it out on the bottom of his shoe before tucking the butt in the back pocket of his black jeans.

For long minutes there was silence. I did the job quickly and efficiently, and I had to give Maksim credit—for this being his first time watching a cleanup, he didn't lose his shit. Maybe he had balls after all.

"You want to hit up Yama? We could check out the fights down below at the Pit? I heard there are a couple of brutal ones booked tonight. Or I heard they got some new girls at Nino's."

I finished cleaning up and glanced at Maksim. "No," was all I said. I had nothing against either place and had in fact fought plenty of times over the years at Yama—the Bratva underground fight ring. And Nino's, one of the many strip clubs owned by the Ruin, wasn't my style.

"Suit yourself," Maksim murmured. "I'm hitting up Nino's then. Those girls are eager to please the right people, if you know what I mean."

The right people meant Maksim could get free ass because he was associated with the Bratva. If they didn't recognize him by face alone, as soon as he took off his shirt, they'd see his tattoos and know who he was affiliated with.

The same as me.

A group of really fucking bad men.

But where some of them might have been redeemable... I was a monster who had a first-class ticket straight to hell.

Besides, I had plans tonight, plans that included me going somewhere I shouldn't, because I wanted to see someone I had no business looking at.

The far-too-innocent brunette who worked at Sal's all-night diner, a diner that was owned by the Bratva to launder their money. And the latter she'd have no fucking idea about. She probably just saw it as another run-down twenty-four-hour diner that catered to drunks, addicts, and those stumbling in after clubbing all night, looking for piss-poor food after everything else was closed.

I shouldn't have been thinking about her, not while I was alone and lying in bed, and sure as fuck not while I was hacking up the bastard spread out on the ground.

But fuck, she'd been on my mind for months, and for a man who wasn't afraid of anything... wanting her terrified the fuck out of me.

3

Galina

If you were lonely enough, it was almost like you were never alone. It was a constant, heavy presence that weighed on you almost like companionship, another person. It was a friend I'd grown very acquainted with as the years dragged on, especially after I moved to Desolation and left Vegas behind.

When I ran. Escaped.

And I'd been living with that dark companion for the last two months. How fitting was it that I'd created a new life in Desolation, NY. A new name. A new background. The lie of my life.

But I couldn't hate Desolation, especially this shitty part of town, especially Sal's diner, where I

waitressed. It was the only place that hadn't asked
me any questions, didn't do a background check,
and paid me under the table.

I stared at the old, faded industrial-looking clock
that hung on the diner wall to my right. I had no
doubt if I pulled it down, it would be coated in an
inch-thick layer of grime. Same with about anything
in this piece-of-shit restaurant.

The time said it was late as hell, or early,
depending on how you wanted to look at it. It was a
little after three in the morning, and fortunately I
only had a couple of hours left on my shift.

I didn't mind the crappy hours or the depressing
aesthetic of Sal's. They gave me as many hours as I
wanted, the tips were decent when I worked the rush
hour, first thing in the morning, and being here kept
me from having to sit in my hole-in-the-wall apartment alone, wondering if they'd find me, if my past
would catch up with me.

I'd heard the backstory of Sal's from Laura, one
of the waitresses who worked the night shift with
me. She told me Sal's had been operating for the last
fifty years and had once been owned by a husband
and wife, Sicilian immigrants who'd gotten their
American dream of owning their own business.

But sadly, when Marianna—the wife—passed

away, her husband Sal had followed not long after. And then, *surprise*, a private organization—AKA no doubt a shady business who was more than likely using this place as a front for money laundering—had swooped in pretty damn fast and taken ownership. I put the latter together myself, given my background with less-than-notable affiliations.

And here I was, two months after running from Henry and his sick plans for me to pay for my father's debt. I was living the dream, let me tell you, but pushing greasy-as-hell burgers, flat colas, and three-day-old apple pie slices to drug addicts, sex workers, drunks, and anyone else who wanted a place to get off the street since we were open twenty-four hours every day of the year was better than the alternative.

I wasn't Galina Michone anymore. I was Lina Michaels. The fake ID had been easy enough to get in Vegas, and my life here in Desolation was eerily similar to being back "home," so I'd assimilated fine.

"Can I get some fucking service over here?"

I exhaled wearily and rubbed my eyes before heading over to the clearly drunk customer who'd just come in. I'd seen him plenty of times before, and he was always obnoxious and demanding—not to mention intoxicated. It was clear he thought women were beneath him by the tone of his voice and the look in his eyes when he addressed the opposite sex. He was like every other asshole I'd come in contact with during my life.

I could smell the booze pouring off him before I even got to his table but tried to put on a professional smile, even if I knew it no doubt looked forced and wouldn't help with this asshole's tipping. Because he never did.

He glared at me, and I pulled my pad and pen out of my apron. "What can I get for you?"

For a second he just stared at me with bloodshot, glossy eyes and a light sheen of sweat covering his forehead, causing his hair to be damp at his hairline. He also smelled like he hadn't washed in a while and had only consumed alcohol for the last twenty-four hours.

"Burger and fries. Beer. And make sure it's cold." He spit out the last word, and I didn't respond, just nodded and turned to leave.

He reached out and snatched hold of my wrist, his grip unyielding. Instantly my defenses went up even more, and my body tightened.

"Make sure my beer is fucking cold." His words were slurred and sloppy, just like his appearance.

"Let go of me," I said low, feigning strength I

didn't feel like I really had. Surprisingly he did without a complaint. I wanted to rub my wrist but didn't want to let him know it bothered me as much as it did. "I'll bring over your stuff shortly. But next time, keep your hands to yourself." I left quickly, not giving him a chance to respond.

After I put in the order, I stood behind the wall, the only privacy I'd get during my shift. Assholes like him didn't bother me so much, not when I'd lived in Vegas and dealt with pricks on the daily. But they still got under my skin at times, now more than ever, and I felt more vulnerable than I had in a long time.

I rested my head on the wall, staring straight ahead at the shelving that held a few supplies. I heard the back door open, and I glanced to the side to see Laura coming through, her tattered island satchel hanging off her shoulder. Her long, dark-blonde ponytail was a little askew as if she'd been running, and when I glanced at the time, I realized she probably had been since she was a few minutes late.

Laura, like me, mainly worked the night shift, but she'd been picking up more hours to save up for classes at the community college. If I had friends, she'd probably be the closest one I'd put that label on.

She glanced up and noticed me, a genuine smile moving over her face. "Sorry I'm late."

I shrugged. What did I care? Things weren't busy right now, and aside from the drunk asshole, there hadn't been much "excitement."

She shrugged out of her jacket and hung it up beside her satchel on the hook that was nailed to the grease-stained wall. She grabbed a "clean" apron, put it on, then stopped in front of me. "The night is that bad already, huh?"

I laughed and shook my head. "Not really. Just the regular drunk asshole."

She screwed up her nose. "Which one? We get so many of them nightly."

So true.

She gave me another smile before exhaling and looked out to the front, her nose wrinkling again. "I have to work a double today. I can't complain, because the tips will probably be good, but Lina... I hate people."

I laughed, the sound shooting out of me before I could stop it. "Same."

We both turned and headed back out to the front. I followed behind, seeing if the drunk was still out there... optimistic that one of these times he'd stumble out and never come back in. But there he was, glaring at the wall, probably thinking of all the ways he could get back at someone who'd wronged him years ago. Because men like him were mean while drunk, but sober... he was probably a nasty bastard.

I was checking to see if his food was ready when I heard the diner's front door open. I glanced over my shoulder, my heart immediately skipping a beat before taking on an erratic note as I watched who walked in. The man was one I'd seen here many times over the past two months.

And he was a man who instantly had every survival instinct in me kicking into gear.

I didn't know him, not his name, age, occupation. He always paid with cash, always kept to himself. He never spoke more than what was required to order his food. And his expression never gave anything away. No frustration, no exhaustion. No pleasure or hatred. Nothing. It was as if he had no emotion, this blank slate that saw nothing but took everything in.

He was tall, with short dark hair, and he carried an air around him that couldn't be mistaken for anything but danger. The power he wielded was breathtakingly clear in just the way he walked, in the way he held himself. And the strength in his body was evident despite the dark clothing that shielded it from view.

But I didn't have to *know* him, didn't have to speak with him to recognize the type of male he was.

Dangerous.

Deadly.

Someone I had no business being curious about.

I'd been around many men like him in my life, men who killed with their hands and moved on to the next task. It was their nature.

I watched him take the same seat he always did, the one at the back of the diner that faced the entrance. He always made sure the wall was at his back. That was another sign of the type of man he was... one who'd seen enough violence that he'd never be caught off guard.

The sound of the cook hitting the little bell, indicating my customer's meal was ready, drew me out of my thoughts. After taking the plate with the burger and fries, I grabbed another beer, noticing how the drunk had already—not surprisingly—drained the first.

I set his plate down in front of him, the beer bottle to follow. He said nothing, just started digging in with disgusting, sloppy sounds leaving him. As soon as I turned and faced the dark and dangerous man sitting in the corner, my belly tightened, that internal warning urging me to run the other way, rising up almost violently.

But I was familiar with that little voice, that sixth sense, and I pushed it down and moved closer. Because although I knew this man was someone I didn't want to get involved with, I also couldn't lie and say my sick curiosity wasn't far stronger.

"Welcome to Sal's," I said automatically. "The usual?" He always got the same. Ham and swiss sandwich on sourdough. Side of fries. Cup of coffee. Black. No sugar.

He nodded, his dark eyes locked on mine, his face giving nothing away. I felt like an animal trapped in a snare and facing off with the hungry predator. I gave a weak nod and an even weaker smile in his direction before I turned and headed toward the cook to put the order in, but I *felt* his gaze still on me, as if he were reaching out and tearing my clothes away, baring my flesh before he took that cold, serrated knife and cut me open.

It was terrifying.

So why did I yearn for more?

4

Arlo

She was demure, innocent, with a soft voice that was pleasing to my ears, a smile that had my chest tightening, and a body that made me want to stab any other man who ever looked her way.

She was dangerous to me, the dark desire I felt, the way she made me want things a bastard like me had no business desiring. And yet I knew nothing about her.

But when I looked into her eyes, I saw a survivor staring back. I was good at reading people without knowing their story. She'd seen the ugliness and violence the world handed out freely... the kind *I* gave in abundance.

Lina, her name tag said, a beautiful name in an ugly city.

I'd come to Sal's plenty of times while living in Desolation, but I couldn't lie and say I didn't come in here almost every fucking night because I wanted to look at her. I wanted to be close to her.

She'd most likely experienced the brutality this world had to offer personally, one that scarred her from the inside out. I felt a tightening in my gut at the strange sensation of wanting to protect her, to save her from further heartache. But who the hell was I to save anyone? I took life. I cleaned up death.

I was a monster wrapped up in the visage of a man. And I shouldn't want to shield her from anything or anyone but me.

I'd made sure to pay her already, wanting her to get her tip and not rely on someone else to hand off Lina's money. Sal's definitely wasn't known for its honor system. I finished my sandwich and coffee, then I waited. I watched. I wanted Lina like a starving wolf seeing a vulnerable lamb. Every part of me looked at her and demanded I take her down to the darkest parts with me, that I destroy her in the best of ways... to tear her apart until I got my fill.

I wasn't sure what it was about Lina that called to me... a more noble part of me, one that had never existed. One that would never be born. All I knew with a harsh truth was that she wouldn't leave my mind. She was a constant companion in my fucked-up head, a light in the blood and murder that took up residence there.

I watched as she handed the check to the piece of shit who'd been loud since I'd come into the diner, her only other customer. I'd seen him before and could always recognize him by the scent of liquor that seeped from his pores.

He squinted at the check, then tossed a few bills on the table despite the waitress holding her hand out for the money. I could see the frustration and almost resignation on her face as she picked up the money, murmured something, and turned to walk off.

Once again, raw anger filled me on her behalf.

My hands were in tight fists on top of the old, chipped two-seater table, the need for bloodshed moving viciously through my veins, all because of the way he glared at her... disrespected her.

And the longer I stared at him, the more I recognized what kind of man he was. I'd seen countless bastards like him before, ones who looked at the women trafficked by the crime syndicate, ones who were sick and needed their dicks cut off because of the perverse things they thought about. And I could see the drunk fucker was hungry for Lina, but the only type of satiation a man like him would get was the kind coming from a begging woman.

I followed Lina with my gaze once more, and I could tell she was trying hard not to look at me by the tension in her shoulders and the way her hands tightly curled inward. Maybe I fascinated her in a sick way. Maybe I scared her so much that she was drawn to me, a girl who'd been damaged enough in her life that I was the only type of man who could pull her out of that darkness.

Because I was as black and cold as the night.

I felt a dangerous coil of... desire move through me. But I knew feelings such as those would do nothing but destroy me. My life, the world I lived in, had no business with something like *that*.

I watched her mannerisms, could see the armor she wore was chinked and scarred, and that made me want to burrow myself deeper under her skin and find out who she was. Where did she come from? Who was she running from?

I'd gotten the basic information on her. Address. Name. Age. The latter two were easily faked, seeing as she had only moved to Desolation in the last couple of months. It could've been easy enough to gather all the information on her that was buried deep... the real information that some people went to a lot of trouble to bury. I definitely had the connections and resources. But something stopped me from searching out information on this woman.

Another uncomfortable, unusual sensation to me. I felt like it would be an invasion of her privacy to delve deeper, not something I'd ever fucking cared about before.

I felt my scowl deepen, hating that she'd worked her way under my skin as swiftly and strongly as she had. I'd never given a shit about what anyone thought or how the outcome would play out. I didn't care how they saw me as long as they knew I was the one to fear.

Right before she rounded the corner and would have disappeared into the back room, she glanced over her shoulder at me. Our eyes locked, hers flaring slightly, because no doubt she hadn't expected me to be watching her so closely. I could practically hear the surprised—maybe frightened— inhalation she took. She was afraid, and rightly —smartly—so.

I could've said I wouldn't hurt her, but she would have known that was a lie. And so would I.

She disappeared behind the door, and I drew my

attention back to the drunk. I could envision myself killing him ten different ways. At the very thought of ending his life, immense satisfaction ran through me. I fantasized about gouging out his eyes for simply looking at the little waitress. He was the type of man who deserved death ten times over for the heinous crimes he'd committed in life.

I should know, because I deserved it as well.

Lina came out a few minutes later, the jacket she wore light blue in color, faded, and older, with one hand tucked into a pocket. She had her backpack slung over her shoulders, her head tipped down, the long fall of her hair shrouding her profile from me.

She quickly made her way through the diner before opening the door and stepping outside, not once looking at me again. Movement to my left had me slowly looking at the drunk. He pulled his stumbling ass out of the booth, his focus on the door Lina had just left out of. Every muscle in my body tightened in preparation to go after him, knowing exactly what he was doing, knowing the opportunity he saw in this moment.

I left the diner, keeping to the shadows once outside, and immediately spotted Lina up ahead. She moved quickly and was scanning her surroundings. *Definitely not a stranger to being on guard.*

But she wasn't alone. I couldn't see him yet, but I felt my skin tightening, a familiar feeling that covered me when I needed to be on alert. And then I saw him, the fucker keeping close to the buildings, staying within the shadows. He stalked her, and even from my vantage point, I could see a tenseness across Lina's shoulders.

She knew she wasn't alone. She could *feel* it. Whether she could see the bastard following her, I didn't know, but I did notice the way she kept her hand in the pocket of her coat. I knew she had a weapon tucked within.

Smart girl.

I crept closer, my muscles even tighter, my body poised to attack. I felt that familiar bloodlust move through me.

Bloodlust—he and I were old friends.

And then the asshole attacked, lunging for Lina and quickly wrapping his arms around her waist as he pulled her into a darkened corner. I picked up my pace to eat the distance and stopped when I rounded the corner of the building. I saw him only a few feet ahead, his hand around her throat, her eyes wide as she clawed with one hand at where he gripped her.

I was about to bash his skull into the side of the brick building when she pulled out a small canister, pointed it at his face, and doused the fucker in the eyes with pepper spray.

He cursed low, a string of profanities as he let her go and stumbled back, his hands frantically wiping away at his face. I was about to attack, when she reared her leg back and kicked him in the balls, making him crumble to the ground.

Fierce, dark desire shot through me at the fight in her, at how she stood up for herself. I felt the stirring of that pleasure in my cock, my breathing increasing, my heart racing. God, she was gorgeous as she stared down at the fucker with this fierceness and need for survival covering her face.

And then she darted off in the other direction, running fast and hard, her steps echoing off the tall buildings until it was just the prick and me in the alleyway.

I curled my hands into tight fists, then relaxed them. I did this over and over again as I moved closer to him. He struggled to stand up, one hand covering his balls, the other palm still wiping away at his eyes. My boot kicked away a stray piece of glass, and he stilled, looking in the direction the sound came from, his body freezing.

"Who's there?" He tried to sound stronger than he was. He reached into his jacket to produce a knife, moving it back and forth in front of him as if that would stop me from what I was about to do.

I kept enough distance to where his blade couldn't touch me, but it wouldn't matter if he did get me. It wouldn't do much damage. My tolerance for pain was so high I wouldn't even feel the blade sinking into my flesh, wouldn't think twice about wrapping my hands around the edge until it dug into my skin, sliced me up, and covered the ground in blood. In fact... I anticipated whatever pain he thought he could inflict.

I looked at his hand that was wrapped tightly around the handle, remembering how he'd curled his fingers around Lina's slender neck. I had no doubt she'd have a mark come morning. And that had my rage intensifying. I'd already decided to kill him, but now I'd make his death excruciating.

In a move so fast he wouldn't have been able to stop me even if he could've seen, I had his knife in my hand and my fingers wrapped around his thick throat. He was strong, even in his intoxicated state. But I was stronger.

The stench of him was overpowering, but I leaned my full weight into his body, bringing us closer, cutting off his airflow until he started clawing at my hand, desperate to suck oxygen into his lungs.

I said nothing. There were no words that needed to be spoken. I was going to take his life as easily as if I blew out a candle, and there was nothing he could do about it. He'd signed his death warrant the moment he looked at Lina. He'd accepted this fact the moment he laid a hand on her.

And I didn't try to sift through why I felt so strongly about this, about her. It was just this feeling that needed to consume me, or nothing was right and good in my life. It was this powerful urge to take out any threat that presented itself to her.

I would be her defender. I would be her assassin.

He started struggling less, his body relaxing farther as he got weaker, as asphyxiation claimed its icy, dark hold on him. I lifted the knife and looked at the blade, the serrated edge gleaming and sharp. This wasn't just a simple weapon. This was a hunting knife, one meant to field dress an animal in the wild.

And I was going to use it on him in the most brutal fashion imaginable.

His gasps were weak but pained, his fear tangible in the air. I let go of his throat and let him crumble to the ground. He gasped louder, already sucking in copious amounts of oxygen. I crouched in front of him, gripped his meaty forearm, and pressed it to the brick of the building.

And then as I looked into his face, his eyes swollen shut from the pepper spray, tears covering his cheeks, sweat coating his forehead, I took that blade and started sawing at his wrist. His cries were loud and would have drawn attention if we weren't in Desolation. But he'd find no hope or rescue in this city. They'd hear his pleas and screams of pain and go in the other direction.

The sound of bone crunching apart from the blade, of flesh being torn away filled my ears. The scent of coppery blood filled my nose, surrounding me in a grizzly depiction of what my life was. Of *who* I was.

His hand fell to the dirty alley ground with a *thud*, spurts of blood spraying out from the stump that topped his forearm, splattering against my hand and arm. He was weeping as if *he* were the victim.

I let go of his wrist and stood, taking a step back and appreciating my work. He cradled his arm to his chest, his tears now from pain and fear. But I wasn't done with him yet.

I reached down and curled my fingers around his neck again, lifting him easily off the ground. He didn't struggle anymore, too weak, too afraid. He kept pleading, kept whimpering.

And still I didn't fucking care.

I wished I could look into his eyes and watch the light fade.

I ran the blade down the center of his chest, causing him to still, to pant. It would be so easy—feel so good—to just sink the knife into his belly and jerk it upward, opening him up so his intestines covered the ground. But instead I placed the tip right over his crotch and watched him hold his breath and freeze.

A slow smile covered my face as adrenaline moved through me even faster. I slammed the blade into his dick and let it sink in just enough before I twisted the handle and jerked it upward, opening up the part he would have used to brutalize Lina.

He screamed and thrashed, a burst of survival energy moving through him. I pulled the knife out and let him go before stepping back, letting him sink to the ground. He'd bleed out soon enough from the arm wound and now what I'd done to his dick.

I bent down to wipe the blood off his blade on his shirt but kept the weapon. I didn't need to wait around to make sure he'd die. The wounds I'd inflicted on him were sufficient, and my knowledge on how to deliver a deathblow was accurate. The fucker would be found at some point, tomorrow no doubt, but it would just be another body found in Desolation with no leads.

When I left the alley, I should have gone home to shower the death and violence off me, but I found myself heading in the opposite direction, toward the one woman I should leave alone.

Five minutes later I stood outside of Lina's apartment building in the shadows and stared up at what I knew was her bedroom window. When I found out her address and what apartment she lived in, I'd walked by more than once. I turned into the stalker I'd never been.

The bass of music came from one of the many dilapidated homes, the scent of stale smoke and car exhaust a constraint in the air. I moved closer to a sparse-looking tree on the verge of dying in the "backyard" of the building.

I made my way to the tree, my focus never leaving Lina's bedroom window. The moon was bright enough that it cast light over the back of the building, allowing me to see her tiny shape moving behind the sheet.

I still held the knife in my palm, had the fucker's blood drying on my hands and clothes. Adrenaline was humming through my veins, a high an addict would kill for.

And they did. *I* did.

I had no business being here, being close to her. I shouldn't have followed her, but I wanted to protect her. I wanted to make sure that her almost assault hadn't hurt her more than I knew about.

I didn't know what was happening to me, and I should have put her behind me as easily as I did everything else. But then this vulnerable, tiny woman had inserted herself into my life unknowingly, crossing paths with the hungry wolf. And as I stood there, wanting nothing more than to go to her, to tell her she was mine, I knew how dangerous that was for her. For me.

I knew how dangerous she truly was to *me*.

And even if I should've left her alone, put her out of my head and my life, I knew the outcome would always be the same.

I'd go to the diner tomorrow night. I'd watch her, talk to her. I couldn't help it, because the truth was, for the first time in my miserable fucking existence, I had a weakness... and that was Lina.

And, God help her, I didn't want to be strong.

5

Galina

I was familiar with fear and the rush of adrenaline. It had been a companion in my life for as long as I could remember. So why was I shaking after my attack? Why was I having trouble breathing at the memory of his hands on my throat? Why was my vision going from clear to fuzzy, making it hard to focus?

I exhaled, shook my head to clear it, and found myself walking around my bedroom, unable to sit still, feeling as if I was missing something, as if there was an integral part of me that I'd left back there in that alley.

In Vegas.

I stopped in the center of my bedroom and looked down at my hands. They still shook slightly, and I scowled at them, curling my fingers tightly until the prick of my nails pressing into my palm had that rage inside me loosening.

Letting fear and the sensation of not having control take over my life wasn't something I'd ever allow, not if I had the power to be strong.

I swallowed, the pain and roughness in my throat a reminder that the asshole'd had his thick fingers digging into my skin, his nails all but tearing at my flesh. I loosened my fingers from the tight cage, went into the bathroom, and turned on the light, the fluorescent bulb above me flickering before finally settling and staying on.

I could hear the electricity moving through the lightbulb, almost loud enough to drown out my warring thoughts.

I curled my fingers around the yellow-colored sink, the entire bathroom like something out of a '70s home interior catalog. I leaned forward, the mirror above me cracked in the corner, spider veins snaking down the edges.

The woman who stared back at me was familiar, yet she was also a stranger. She was used to the horrors of life. But as I looked into my blue eyes, I could see the truth. I was empty. I'd been that way for a very long time.

For some reason I thought back to the dark-haired man in the diner. His gaze made something warm and unusual grow within me, his focus so strong that I felt it as if he were reaching through the distance and pulling me in close. It was crazy, unrealistic, and so very dangerous. I couldn't entertain the idea of making any kind of connections like that. I couldn't allow myself to be *known* like that.

My gaze went down to my throat, where four finger-sized bruises were starting to form on one side, and a thumbprint mark on the other. I looked at my hands, hating that they still shook, and lifted my fingers to touch the marks.

Although my throat was raw and tender, I didn't feel much of anything else.

Am I dead inside?

Was this what it meant to only survive, not live?

I went through the motions of getting ready for bed before leaving the bathroom and heading back into my bedroom. Although I hadn't eaten anything since early this afternoon, I had no appetite, my stomach feeling like it had a stone lodged in the center.

I stood in the doorway of the bedroom and

stared at the mattress with no frame pushed up against the corner wall. This apartment was disgusting, far worse than the last hole-in-the-wall place I'd been in when I was in Vegas. But it was this type of place that would protect me from the people I ran from. It was a place to keep me hidden.

It was places like this, places that were in shit parts of cities, that didn't require background checks or credit approvals. They took cash in the palm of their hands and asked no questions when I handed them my fake ID. As long as I paid on time every month, I was left alone.

Aside from the mattress, the room was barren, not even a dresser. But I didn't need nor want furniture. I didn't want to get settled, because this place wasn't a home. I kept my clothes in my backpack, always carrying it with me in case I had to run again.

I walked over to the window and pulled the old, pale-yellow sheet aside. It had been the only other thing in the bedroom besides the mattress, and I used it as a makeshift curtain, although I was pretty sure people could still see through it at the right angle.

The scent of age and musk filled my nose, this uncomfortable tingle in my sinuses.

My apartment was only one story up, something

I was very thankful for in case I had to run again, in case my only exit was this window. I stared out at the neighborhood. It was just as depressing and dirty, gloomy and dark as you'd expect in a city that was filled with addicts and crime.

The houses that were in this part of town were small two-story, bungalow-style homes, but they weren't *homes* at all. They were four walls and a roof, privacy for people to inject and snort, rape, and murder.

There were a few businesses within walking distance of me. A deli that sold questionable meat and delivered an even worse atmosphere. There was a laundromat just down the block, and a check-cashing place on the other end of the street. A pizza joint was close as well, and a small convenience store across from that. So although the neighborhood was run-down and barely thriving, it gave me enough of the amenities I needed in order to survive.

I let my gaze travel over what might have once been a lush expanse of grass for children to play on but had long since died and was now nothing more than yellow and crispy patches trying to hang on to that last hope of staying alive.

There was one tree, but it was even sadder than the decrepit neighborhood, with barely any leaves hanging onto the skeletal branches, its thirst evident in the gnarled trunk. It was as dead as everything else in Desolation.

The shadows were dark and thick at the back of the building, and the few streetlights that lined the road had long since given up. And of course the city couldn't care less about fixing them, so they continued to let the depression cave in around people.

I felt this tingling on the back of my neck, something I was very familiar with, a feeling that told me I was being watched. I should've moved away from the window, allowed this dirty sheet to give me a semblance of privacy I desperately wanted in life, but I found myself rooted to the spot. I looked, searching for who was out there. But there was nothing to see but the sadness, ugliness, and the forever darkness.

One day I'd be able to feel safe. One day I'd be able to make a home and be happy.

But that day wasn't today.

6

Galina

I'd been at work for the last two hours, and there was an unusual rush this time of night that kept me busy, which I was thankful for. It helped keep my mind off the night before and what had happened.

I felt someone come up behind me before the scent of Laura's too strong, flowery perfume filtered in my nose.

"Hey," she said, and there was something off about the tone of her voice.

I turned around from restocking the Styrofoam cups to look at her. "Everything okay?" The expression on her face answered my question. She had her brows pulled down low and slowly shook her head as if clearing her thoughts.

When she looked up at me, I could see dark circles under her eyes before her gaze took in my throat. Her eyes widened, and she moved a step closer. "Oh my God. What happened?"

Instinctively I touched my neck where I knew the marks were. I'd bought some cheap concealer, but the shade wasn't a match and made the bruising look even worse. I shook my head and said, "It's nothing. Just someone too touchy-feely. I doused him with my pepper spray and kicked him in the balls to teach him a lesson." I gave her a smile that I felt wavering and didn't reach my eyes. She looked like she wanted to argue, but I shook my head. "I'm fine. Promise. Now tell me what's going on with you."

After a moment, when it was clear I wouldn't budge on this, she exhaled and tied her apron around her waist before leaning back and resting her hands behind her on the chipped counter.

"Well, if you don't count the fact that I'm barely scraping by moneywise, or that my dreams of getting a college education are slowly slipping through my fingers, then yeah, I'm doing great, all things considering." She laughed humorlessly, and although I knew I should comfort her, it was never something I'd had experience with.

I reached out and placed my hand on her shoulder, and she looked up at me, her light-brown eyes showing me how tired she really was. I wished I could've told her things would be okay, but the truth was nothing was ever okay in the world we lived in.

I wished I could have helped her with the money aspect, but I was barely making enough to support myself and save up to leave. I was struggling just as badly as she was, and that wasn't even counting the shitstorm of my past that would catch up with me eventually.

Laura didn't even know who I *really* was.

What I didn't spend on food and necessities, I squirreled away. Desolation certainly wasn't my endgame. I didn't want to spend the rest of my life here. I wanted to be able to go somewhere that was full of life. Because maybe then I would actually feel like I had one.

But the cherry on the shit sundae that was my life story was that they'd found a body just down the street from where I worked. Although finding corpses in this city wasn't exactly breaking headliner news, there was a prickling on my skin that told me this wasn't just *any* death.

"So that body they found?"

"Yeah?" I waited to see if she'd give more information or if I'd have to press a little harder. I didn't watch the news and didn't want to be any more depressed than I was. And the news that tended to be throughout Desolation was always the same. Warring criminal factions, gang wars, deaths from either murder or drug addiction. And of course there was rape and sexual assault.

She leaned in close and looked around as if she was afraid someone would hear, although nobody that frequented cared. In fact, they probably had a hand in many of the news stories that had come out over the years.

"This isn't public knowledge, not yet anyways, but I have a friend who works at the local paper who has connections with a guy who works at the police station. Apparently the body they found not only had his hand cut off, but he also had a wound on his..." She pointed down to her crotch region. "The wound was so substantial that he bled out from the groin before he could from the missing hand."

My heart jumped in my throat at the brutality of his death.

The front door opened, and we both looked toward the entrance. My heart, that had been beating fast and erratic from Laura's story, stilled in my chest at the sight of the man who stepped in. The same man who consumed my thoughts and made me question what was going on with my body for the last two months.

He took his usual seat, but I didn't miss how he kept his gaze locked on mine.

"Why is he watching you so—"

"Yeah," I said before she could finish. "It's intense." I glanced away, because his eyes on me were heavy, so heavy it was like a cloak over me.

But I found myself looking back at him. I didn't miss how his gaze moved down to my throat, didn't miss the way his jaw tightened as he no doubt saw the marks. I forced myself not to touch my neck, feeling bared even from across the restaurant.

"Yeah, he screams, 'Stay the hell away.'"

I snapped my attention toward Laura and saw that she was staring at him, but she quickly looked away. I didn't miss how she shivered and then shook her head, her focus on her hands.

"He looks at you like he wants to eat you up until there's nothing left," she whispered before clearing her throat and pushing away from the counter. "There's just something about him that scares the hell out of me." Her voice was soft, and she finally looked up at me before slapping on a smile, which I could tell was forced. "But the men I've been around and this shitty city have kind of ruined it for all others."

This would've been a good time for us to bond, for me to tell her she wasn't alone, that I, too, knew all about bad men. But she was gone before I could say anything. I didn't even know if I would have been able to say anything. Connecting with people wasn't a strong suit of mine.

I looked back at him and gathered my strength. I made my way over to him, his eyes never leaving me, as if he were the negative end of a magnet and I the positive. I was drawn to him, this invisible thread that was winding tighter the closer I got.

When I was right in front of his table, I held the pad in one hand and a pen in the other. My fingers shook, and I tightened them around the objects. His gaze flickered down, and I knew he saw my physical nervousness. I had a feeling he could read me better than I could read myself.

When he was looking back at me, I felt my tongue swell, my throat tighten, that pain from being strangled last night making itself known once more. As if he knew the latter, his focus once more lingered on my neck. Although his outward appearance seemed stoic, almost uncaring, I noticed a slight, subtle clench of his jaw, the same thing when he first looked at the bruising.

I found myself fidgeting with my hair, pulling it over my shoulders to hide the marks. There was nothing I could do about them, but I certainly didn't want anyone paying attention to the marks either. "The usual?" I hated that my voice was so low, slightly shaky. And it didn't have anything to do with anxiety.

Why was I so on edge around him right now? All the other times, I'd been able to at least pretend like his presence didn't rattle me. Maybe it was the way he stared at me, his dark eyes so intent and prying, as if he could sift through my darkest secrets and find out exactly *who* I was without me uttering a word.

"Lina, right?" He looked down at my name tag, and I nodded, licking my lips. He was staring at my mouth now, and I felt an intense flush cover my face at the fact that he watched me so hard. There was something behind his gaze, something that wasn't apathetic. Something that was... heated.

And I felt an answering call from my body. It was uncomfortable and unusual.

It was exhilarating.

It was the first time I felt anything but the lonely despair that had always been crushing me.

"Yes," I said with a stronger voice this time. "That's what the name tag says," I teased and offered him a smile, but he didn't give me one in return. Which then had mine dying a slow, embarrassing death. "So." I cleared my throat again. "The usual?"

He was silent for so long I wondered if he'd heard me. Had I said the words out loud or thought them? I certainly didn't want to ask again and further embarrass myself. Maybe I should just turn and give him the space he clearly needed.

"I'm Arlo," he finally said, and I felt my eyes widen at the piece of information he gave me. Because for some reason he seemed like a man who didn't give anyone *any* part of himself. "Arlo Malkovich."

I nodded slowly, not sure what to say, but then common sense kicked in, and I replied, "Lina Michaels."

He leaned back in the chair and regarded me. "Lina Michaels."

The way he said it made me feel as if I'd been caught evading the truth. Of course it was a lie, but if he was calling me out, he didn't blatantly do it. I licked my lips again and nodded, not trusting my voice.

He tipped his chin in my direction. "What happened to your neck?"

There was this weird tone in his voice, as if he knew the answer to that question already. But clearly he couldn't have known the truth. I'd left while he'd still been finishing his meal, and my assailant had taken me into an alley. It had just been him and me until I left him clutching his family jewels and ran.

I found myself making sure my hair was still covering my neck before I shook my head. "Nothing. Just an unfortunate event." I cleared my throat and started shifting on my feet, not liking the way his look made me feel.

But fortunately he didn't press for more answers. I didn't know why he even asked about my neck in the first place. It was very clear by his stoic expression he didn't care one way or another.

"You come here quite frequently." I could have slapped a hand over my mouth at what just came from me.

One of his dark eyebrows crept up ever so slightly, as if he was surprised I'd been so forward with my statement.

"I do," he said slowly, evenly.

Tonight he wore a dark jacket, a white pressed shirt underneath. He looked more like a businessman than somebody who should be dining in the middle of the night at Sal's.

I could see tattoos that crept up from underneath the collar of his shirt along the base of his throat. I could even see some on his wrists that also marked the back of his hands. I wondered how much more of him was covered in ink.

"Yes, the usual, Lina."

The way he said my name sent a visible shiver through me. And it was very clear by his expression that he didn't miss it.

My pulse was rushing through my ears, so I couldn't think clearly, let alone speak. I forced myself to turn around and walk toward the back to put his order in, and once again, the entire time, I felt his gaze on me.

Who was this man? What was he to me? And how was I going to handle it?

7

Arlo

After I left Sal's, I knew exactly where I *needed* to go.

Yama, or the Pit as it was called in English, was like a split personality. One where, on the surface, you had something pretty, something tolerable. Socially acceptable. Beautiful women, exotic drinks, an atmosphere expensive and pleasing to the eye. A man could get his wildest fantasies fulfilled in the rooms above.

But then there were the bowels of Yama. The pit of hell itself. And inside that was so deep and dark not even light penetrated.

And for a long time the Pit had been the only

way for me to diminish some of the darkness that lived inside me.

The killing, the cleaning and fixing for the Ruin, for the Bratva, did help satiate all the heinous shit I felt deep down. Having somebody to go up against, someone who had the strength and agility, the same evilness lurking in them and willingness to give it back tenfold, was a whole different kind of fight.

It was the hits to my body, that pain wrapped up in brutality, that made me feel something other than the brokenness that shaped the man I was today.

And it was in this sphere where the bloodthirsty anger of what made a person survive came to the surface. It came alive, growing until it threatened to swallow you whole. And then you unleashed it within the metal cage, letting that blood and flesh cover your chest and soak the ground, a visual that you were strong, that you were here, that no one and nothing could take you down.

It meant you were *real.*

I sat on a small, bloodstained wooden bench in the corner of the cage and focused on my taped hands, my fingers extending and contracting as I flexed them. I hadn't been to the Pit in several months, not feeling that darkness creep up on me.

But ever since that all-consuming desire for Lina

arose, I'd felt myself starting to unravel, to fray around the edges as it spread outward until I'd be nothing but tatters on the ground.

The need to possess her had started to control me. And that was a very dangerous situation. I'd never given any part of myself to another person, never allowed anyone to have that kind of control over me.

So this was what I needed, to brutally destroy, to feel pain... to allow someone to give it to me.

And then my opponent stepped into the cage, a six-foot-five hulking beast who went by the Russian name Razoreniye. Or was simply known as *Ruin* in English. A killer for the Bratva, a man who was darker and deadlier than even me. He had no mercy, no empathy... nothing holding him back from being as dark as he wanted.

And he was exactly the man I wanted to fight tonight. He'd be as violent toward me as I would be toward him.

And right now I needed that more than anything.

He stepped in close, the lifelike wolf head tattoo covering the entire front part of his chest and other Bratva insignia inked on his big body.

The sounds of the bastards thirsty for the blood

that would spill rang through the room. Bids for who would win this fight were shouted out in Russian, the words flowing together so they all sounded like the same string of notes through my head.

I stood, rolling my head around my neck, adrenaline making my muscles feel bigger, more powerful. If Razoreniye could have smiled in sadistic pleasure, I was sure he'd do it now. As it was, we both faced off, neither of us giving anything away.

And when the bell rang, all hell broke loose.

We were two tornadoes slamming into each other, fists a blur, the punches coordinated, the pain a welcome retreat. I absorbed it all, letting Razoreniye hit me more times than I'd ever allow another person to. And it was because that was the only way my inner war was tamed.

The only way I could gather any kind of fucking control.

I HAD A BUSTED LIP, a cut above my eye, and the dark pleasure of the relief I'd yearned for coursing through me as I left Yama and stepped out into the night, cold fall night of Desolation, New York. The feeling of my cell vibrating in my coat pocket had me

reaching inside and pulling it out as I made my way
toward my Mercedes.

I didn't recognize the number that flashed across
the screen, but it would have only been someone
close to me, or the Ruin, as no other soul would have
had this number.

I hit Accept and put the phone to my ear, not
saying anything. Whoever it was could either start
speaking or hang up after all they heard was
dead air.

"We need your assistance, Arlo." The deep voice
was instantly recognizable. "We need your help with
a cleanup."

Twenty minutes later I pulled to a stop in front of
Butcher and Son, a decades-old abandoned slaughterhouse on the outskirts of Desolation. I parked my
Mercedes and let the headlights illuminate the large
bay doors. Although I didn't see any other vehicles, I
knew what waited for me inside.

After killing the engine and getting out, I
scanned my surroundings, my hand tucked into the
inner pocket of my jacket and my fingers wrapping
around the grip of my gun.

When I was confident I was alone, I went to the
trunk, grabbed my duffel that held the basic supplies

I'd need to clean up the body, and made my way toward the slaughterhouse.

Once inside, the scent of age and mold slammed into my sinuses. My vision adjusted to the darkness, and I searched the large interior of Butcher and Son. I spotted the corpse in the corner, but the dark shape not far from it had my body coming even more alert.

With my hand back on the grip of the gun, I moved toward the two bodies. It was when I was a few feet away that I stopped and focused my attention on one of the men lying supine on the slaughterhouse floor.

Stone. Another associate of the Ruin. And he was alive. *Really fucking interesting turn of events.*

If I were a man who could be surprised, this would have been one of those times. As it was, I felt nothing but annoyance that this wouldn't be an easy, quick fix like I planned, and instead I'd deal with two bodies instead of one.

Stone was a man I didn't know much about, but one who was just as connected with the Ruin as I was. Although he and I weren't friends and had no connection other than the same crime syndicate, we'd crossed professional paths more than once, and I did hold mild respect for him because of that.

I didn't see him as even an acquaintance, but he

also wasn't my enemy, and because of the latter, I'd help get him the fuck out of here instead of killing him. Because if he were anyone else, any other poor bastard who was in the wrong place at the wrong time and allowed themselves to be vulnerable, I'd get rid of them so there wasn't even more fallback.

Stone was lying on the ground, the corpse not far from him. If I hadn't seen Stone's chest rise and fall, I might have taken his otherwise still body as being long dead.

When I was beside him, I crouched and just stared at him for a moment. I didn't know what the fuck had gone down here for Stone to even be in this situation, nor did I care. He needed out so I could get my shit done.

I said in a low, deep voice, "Wake up, dumbass." He didn't respond, and I said louder, "Open your eyes." Stone groaned, and a moment later he obeyed, his eyes opening and the fuzziness in the dark depths fading as the seconds moved by and he got his bearings. "Come on, time for you to get the fuck gone, Stone."

"Arlo?" he prompted gruffly before coughing, blood spraying from his lips and covering my shirt with red droplets.

I glanced down at the blood on my white shirt

that looked black on the material from the ominous lighting. *Fucking perfect.* "Come on," I said again and helped him off the ground. "Let's get you out of here so I can do my job."

Stone didn't say anything as he looked at my face, his gaze taking in the busted lip and cut above my eye.

"What the fuck?" he grunted out.

I didn't bother responding to the clear fact that I'd gotten in a fight. If you were part of the Ruin, you knew not to ask too many questions.

He braced his weight against me. "But how? Why?"

I didn't know if he'd been hit over the head and that's why he kept running his mouth, but I helped him out of the warehouse. Maybe some fresh air would clear his mind. "See, those are questions. And I don't want fucking questions."

"I don't understand."

I wasn't sure what he was going on about, most likely private business. Either way, not my concern. Stone rested against the side of the slaughterhouse, and I grabbed my cell. After a quick call to the Ruin for a pickup, I disconnected the call and shoved my cell back in my pocket. I knew whoever wanted

Stone dead would want confirmation, but that wasn't my fucking concern.

Ten minutes later a car's headlights flashed, and the vehicle was coming to a stop beside us.

"Just get the fuck out of here, Stone. You want to survive? Leave."

He nodded. "But what about you?"

I shook my head and said nothing. I stared him in the eyes, seeing what a hardheaded bastard he was.

I ran a hand over my face, feeling a rush of pleasure when my palm scraped over my busted lip.

"Thanks." He opened the back passenger-side door.

I tipped my head in acknowledgment. Fortunately he didn't say anything else, just sat in the back and shut the door.

I stood there and watched him leave, pissed that my otherwise "normalcy" of a fix had been met with extra strings tonight.

When the car was long gone, the cloaking darkness closing in on me once more, I turned and headed back inside, about to do what I did best.

Surround myself in everything fucked up.

8

Galina

I curled my fingers around the edge of the newspaper, trying to stop my hands from shaking, but it was a losing battle. The black-and-white picture and headline started to run together the longer I stared at them. It was as if what I was looking at mocked me, reminding me that my life had never been easy, that I'd never get the happily ever after I'd read about in books.

Michael Boyd. Thirty-nine years old. Convicted sexual assault and rape felon. Multiple drug counts. Two probation violations. Details not being released as of now, but homicide is being looked into.

THE PICTURE I currently looked at was the same drunk who'd accosted me in the alley. It was a mug shot, one where he looked just as deranged as he had every time I'd seen him in the diner. I closed my eyes and breathed out slowly as memories of that night in the alley played back. With it only being a couple of days since the attack, it was still very fresh, but all my life, I'd learned how to bury those feelings, that fear and anxiousness, the heavy weight that could make you suffocate.

"It's crazy, right?"

I opened my eyes and blinked a few times to look at Laura, who stood beside me. She was staring at the newspaper, her brows pulled low.

"Crazy?" Was she talking about the fact that it was a murder so close, or because she recognized him? I knew she'd seen him harass me. It was hard to miss when he was loud and obnoxious and didn't exactly hide that he was an asshole whenever he'd come in.

She tipped her chin toward the paper. "That's the

same asshole who came in here and was a prick to you. I remember what a bastard he was. I can't say he didn't get what he deserved." She pointed to the charges he'd been convicted of.

"Yeah," I said softly and folded the paper up before shoving it under the counter. I didn't want to look at it anymore. Laura blinked a few times as if pulling herself out of her own thoughts.

"I really hate this fucking city most days."

I snorted. "Most days?"

She gave me a tight nod. "Ninety-nine percent of the time, okay."

I laughed softly. I'd only been here a couple of months, and I despised everything Desolation stood for. The only positive thing about this hell was that it helped keep me hidden.

"Anyway," she said. "Good riddance."

I couldn't help but smile warily. I was tired, just really damn tired. I wanted to save up as much as I could so I could move to a better place, a place where I'd reinvent myself, a place where the past wasn't always chasing me.

But that seemed like such a pipe dream and not at all realistic. The truth was I'd probably be dead before my twenty-fifth birthday, and that was being optimistic.

"So..."

The way she paused made me think she was hesitant to ask me whatever was on her mind.

"Total subject shift, but you want to make a little —easy—extra money?"

My interest was instantly piqued, as if she'd read my mind on needing money to get out of here. But my hesitance had risen instantly. Earning money was never easy.

"You wouldn't have to do anything illegal, nothing depraved or that goes against your moral compass." She laughed a little, but it wasn't forced.

"I'm listening," I said slowly, cautiously.

"So I waitress at this bar sometimes, and they're looking for a couple of extra hands." When I didn't say anything, she continued, "It's that Russian bar called *Sdat'sya*." I shrugged, never having heard of it. "They are short-staffed, and it's basically just serving drinks to a bunch of old, rich, Russian businessmen."

Old, *rich*, and *businessmen* all in the same sentence would always have warning bells going off.

"The tips are incredible, especially the drunker they get," she teased. "One time I made over five hundred in just a night."

I would've said no right away, simply because a

lot of red flags shot up when I thought about going to some obscure bar and serving drinks to old, rich men. But the money aspect had me not declining right away. "So what's the catch?"

She grimaced. "Sometimes, they can get a little handsy. But they have staff—bouncers, I guess— who have always made sure nothing gets out of hand. Not unless you want to make a little *extra* money." She lifted her eyebrows.

Sex for money was what she implied. I slowly shook my head. "I'm not a prostitute, Laura."

She shook her head. "Neither am I. I'm just saying that's some of the stuff you could see— exchanging of money and... yeah, all that."

Now it was my turn to grimace at the thought of crusty old men trying to cop a feel or worse, thinking I'd put out.

"I don't want to pressure you, but I know you need the money just like me." At my no doubt surprised look, she snorted and shook her head. "Come on, you don't have to actually *tell* me you need money for me to know. You live in Desolation. Enough said."

True enough. Although she'd mentioned at one point the possibility of us living together, I didn't know what my future held. And with Henry and his thugs no doubt coming after me at some point, I didn't want Laura thrown in that mix and dragged down.

I couldn't deny it. She was right, of course. But I had to weigh the pros and cons of putting myself in a position where things could escalate and worsen.

"I just wanted to offer it to you. We are there to serve drinks, not give handjobs... not unless you want," she said on a laugh, and I couldn't help the way my lips twitched in amusement.

A little sliver of reality interjected itself into my thoughts because I knew I couldn't afford to pass up an opportunity like this. I never got chances to supplement my income. And to be honest, any extra income was better than nothing. I'd be closer to leaving Desolation. And maybe if I did a good enough job, they'd let me work other nights there.

"Okay," I said, and she grinned wider. "I don't have anything nice to wear though."

She waved off my words. "No worries. They keep a wardrobe, because they prefer the waitresses to wear certain things to keep up with the aesthetics of the place."

I was feeling a little less sure about this. What kind of place was this where they had expendable clothing all because they wanted to keep up appearances? I understood uniforms, but I doubted this place gave everyone the same drab apparel, especially if they catered to rich and powerful men.

I should've just assumed the night in question would probably end up coming back to bite me in the ass. That's usually how the events in my life went. But beggars couldn't be choosers.

And I was absolutely a beggar at this point.

I'D LEFT work twenty minutes ago, making quick time as I walked the dark, septic streets of Desolation. I'd been convinced someone would attack again, but fortunately aside from a few catcalls, I was left relatively alone.

Once I was inside my apartment building, I still didn't let go of my canister of pepper spray. The sun would be rising soon, my feet ached, and my head hurt, but I couldn't wholly complain. I'd made decent tips and even snagged some food from the diner so I wouldn't go to bed hungry and wouldn't have to stop at the convenience store for some prepackaged shit. And I had a job lined up that would—hopefully—make me some decent money.

I started taking the narrow, trash-laden stairs, the

scent of stale cigarette smoke, old liquor, and the
remnants of what was probably piss and vomit
lingering in the air. I could hear the heavy bass of
rap music playing from one of the apartments on an
upper level. A couple was fighting loudly, and in
another, there was the sound of glass breaking—
normalcy in this building.

Once I got to the landing of the floor my apartment was on, I took a moment to catch my breath
before I made my way to my front door.

I rounded the corner, and my steps faltered
slightly when I saw my neighbor leaning against the
interior frame of his door. A cloud of smoke filled his
apartment and spilled out into the hallway, a dirty
haze that made my vision slightly fuzzy. He brought
his cigarette to his lips and took a long drag from it
as he stared at me, the small cloud of smoke leaving
his mouth as he exhaled.

He wore a stained, what was once probably
white T-shirt, dark pit stains under the arms, a
brown ring painting the collar, and a slight gut
protruding from underneath the otherwise stretched
material. His jeans looked like they hadn't been
washed since he got them, and his feet were bare, his
toenails too long and too yellow. And the entire time

he had his focus latched on to me like a damn leech, refusing to let go.

I averted my gaze quickly and stopped at my door, fumbling with my key for a second before I pushed it into the lock and opened the door. I shut it behind me, turned the deadbolt, and slipped the chain lock in place, then leaned against it.

The domestic shouting sounded louder and right down the hall, and I closed my eyes and thought about what it would be like to be someone else.

But fantasies weren't real. They were fine when you thought you could escape, but once reality slammed back in, that pain was even stronger than before.

9

Galina

The cab pulled to a stop in front of the bar where Laura had told me to meet her. She'd said to be here at ten, which might have seemed late as hell to start a shift, but when you were in the city, it was when the darkness really settled in that life started to come alive.

"We're here," the cab driver said in a thick Eastern European accent. I handed him the amount it cost for the trip, an expense I normally wouldn't have spent, given the fact that I was trying to save up, but I wasn't about to hike it across town at this hour. Going a few blocks from Sal's to my apartment was one thing. Walking to this bar would have been suicide.

I climbed out, and as soon as the cab door was shut, it drove away. *No changing my mind now.*

I tipped my head back and took in the three stories of the building in front of me. The entire structure was black brick, with twin black vinyl doors situated front and center and a small light illuminating it. Compared to all the other buildings on this block, it looked totally out of place.

The sign above the door was red neon and spelled out *Sdat'sya.*

I pulled out my cell phone and sent a quick text to Laura to let her know I was here. Aside from meeting at this place at ten, she hadn't given me any other instructions.

I wasn't brave enough to go through those front doors, which by the way were unguarded. Part of me felt a little bit of trepidation about what lay on the other side, as if I'd be walking into hell itself.

I wasn't stupid in not assuming a lot of Desolation was controlled and owned by the crime syndicate. I knew in Vegas the Italian mafia had a large hand in things. In fact, many cities around the US probably ran the same way. It was just how the

world worked, how things were done. And so I tried
to keep my head down and my business to myself.

Of course, sometimes that shit hits you right in
the face anyway, and there was no trying to come out
without being scarred.

Because the powerful controlled the powerless.

So the fact that this particular building, which
screamed money and had a illicit air to it, not to
mention was obviously Russian owned, told me it was
probably controlled by the Russian mafia. The Bratva.

I looked down the street to my left, then to my
right. A police car slowly drove toward me, and I
stepped farther back, the cold stone wall of the
building stopping my retreat. I knew enough about
law enforcement in cities like this, ones that were
corrupt and twisted, where criminals had the final
say and money could buy anyone and anything.

So the men, the law—who would be the likely
prospect when you needed something or when
running or hiding or begging for sanctuary—they
weren't the ones you'd ask for help. They were the
type of men who took cash in back alleys and looked
the other way. They were the type of men you ran
from. Fast and without looking over your shoulder,
because they'd be right behind you.

And as the police cruiser slowed to a crawl as it passed me, the driver glancing in my direction, his grin was big, with all white teeth in a shadowy interior.

A shiver worked through me despite the still air. I wrapped my jacket tighter around me and watched the cruiser disappear down the street.

A second later my phone vibrated with an incoming text, and I looked down to see Laura's message.

Give me a sec. I'll bring you in.

I tucked my phone back into my jacket pocket, and a moment later I heard footsteps coming from the side. Laura stepped out from the corner of the building and searched around before her gaze settled on me. She smiled and gestured for me to follow her.

Once I was beside her, we headed down a barely lit alley. "Are you sure about this?" I couldn't help asking as I looked around the dumpster- and trash-filled alley.

"It's safe. Don't worry. The crime around here is nonexistent." She snorted as if she knew why. I certainly knew the answer to why no one fucked with this place. *The mafia.*

Even criminals knew when they shouldn't fuck with the big boys.

We only walked a handful of seconds before she stopped in front of a rust-colored metal door. She pounded on it a couple of times before stepping back. It swung open, the metal hinges creaking loudly and echoing off the buildings.

A big, burly guy with not much of a neck and a jagged scar slashed down the side of his face held the door open. I looked at him hesitantly, his expression closed off and slightly dangerous.

I quickly glanced forward and followed Laura inside. When we entered the anteroom, the door closed behind us with a loud *bang*, loud enough that I jumped slightly. I blamed my frazzled nerves on the foreign terrain I was currently embarking in, but the truth was closer to the fact that this entire situation just didn't sit well with me.

And that was probably because I knew the person or people who owned this place weren't good men. *And those are the ones I'm trying to stay away from.*

"Don't worry about Boris," Laura said and looked over her shoulder. "The doorman." She tipped her chin to the burly, scar-faced guy. "He's harmless. At least I assume he is. He rarely speaks and just kind of hangs around in the background. Or he does whenever I've worked."

I looked over my shoulder at Boris, a big, hulking shadow behind us. I faced forward quickly, no doubt in my mind that this man was the *furthest* thing from "not dangerous" as you got.

The anteroom and hallway opened into a larger room, where a handful of girls looked through racks of clothing.

Laura stopped and turned to face me so suddenly that I stumbled back. "What?" I looked around, thinking I'd made some faux pas and hadn't realized. She didn't speak right away and started biting her lip. "Laura, just say it."

"So you have the waitressing job, but the owner of the bar wants to meet you to decide which room to put you in for the night."

I furrowed my brow. "Which room to *put* me in for the night?"

"Yeah." She kept biting her lip. "It's how it works. The way this bar is set up, there are several rooms, kind of like tiers on where the clientele lands. The higher the tier, the more important the patrons."

I nodded slowly. "Okay. So if you're not up to the owner's physical standard, you're shit out of luck and get a bottom level?"

At least she had the decency to flush as she nodded. "I know how it seems, but no matter what, the waitresses still bring home good money, even at the lowest level."

"So we might not even be working in the same room?"

She shook her head and looked apologetic. Not that it mattered if we were in the same room, but I would have preferred a familiar face. Not to mention she'd acted like we would be together because she didn't want to do it alone.

It seemed a little bit strange to me, but I wasn't going to complain about how a business was. This made me feel like, if I was given a lower-end room, clearly the owner didn't like the way I looked. I told myself it really didn't matter in the long run.

Money was money, and I desperately needed it.

Laura gave me a reassuring smile, then eyed me up and down. "Let's get you changed first and do your hair and makeup."

Hair and makeup?

Before I could complain about needing to be dolled up to sling drinks, I told myself getting prettied up would help with tips. Rich old men, especially ones who were drinking copious amounts of booze, tended to throw money at women who caught their eye. Not that I liked it, but it was a fact in the world, and I'd use it to my advantage.

I was just going through the motions as I stood there and let Laura pick out a dress for me. It was white and slinky, covering up the important parts but showing enough that it didn't leave much to the imagination.

"Seriously?" I asked as she handed it to me. "And white?"

She shrugged but smiled. "Trust me, the whole white-young-and-innocent thing will help with tips. This is old rich men we are talking about."

I was already regretting this.

Ten minutes later I was dressed, my hair styled in a soft updo, little wisps framing my face, and a light layer of makeup put on. I stared at myself in the mirror, and although I recognized the woman looking back at me, she also seemed like a stranger. This wasn't who I was. *This is for the endgame. Save money and get the hell out of here.*

I exhaled and was handed a pair of stilettos, which I grudgingly took and slipped on. I looked down at my feet, praying I could not only walk but carry drinks at the same time.

"Gorgeous," Laura said, and I glanced at her reflection in the mirror. "Ready?"

I turned to look at her. She was beautiful as well, with a bloodred dress that ended midthigh and had a slit up the side. She was well-endowed in the chest department—unlike me—and the dress accentuated her breasts.

We left the dressing room and walked down a short hallway before she stopped in front of a closed door. I didn't miss how Boris followed us, an uncomfortable shadow right behind me. After three heavy knocks, a deep voice called out in another language from the other side of the door.

Boris moved in front of Laura and opened the door before stepping aside and letting us in. Laura went in first, me following behind and feeling awfully bare all of a sudden, which had nothing to do with what I wore. The room wasn't overly large, but it was exquisitely decorated. Black leather, sleek dark woods, and very obvious Russian-themed decor.

There was a massive, intimidating desk that sat across from the door, and the man perched behind and the look on his face instantly had warning bells going crazy in my head. My throat tightened at the dark power that clearly surrounded him.

To his right there was a large fireplace, the flames flickering over the faux logs. A black leather couch was situated in front of it and taken up by two men who looked about my age. They were similar in appearance and build, so I was safe to assume they were related to not only each other, but the man behind the desk as well. One of the men, the older of the two, brought a square-cut glass to his mouth, his eyes locked on me as he took a slow sip. A shiver moved up my spine, and I tried to suppress it before turning my attention to the man behind the desk.

Boris said nothing and stepped aside so the man behind the desk could get a good look at Laura and me. She seemed relaxed enough, but I felt this uncomfortable pressure surrounding me all of a sudden. The man didn't hide how he blatantly checked us out.

His eyes seemed very dark—and not in the aspect of color. They just appeared closed off from the world, maybe even his humanity. He leaned back slowly, his leather chair making a soft sound from the shift of weight. For a long second no one spoke as he looked between Laura and me. And then he started speaking in Russian, his voice a smooth, deep timbre.

When the man behind the desk stood, I took an involuntary step back at his size. I immediately regretted showing this weakness and fear, because it didn't go unseen by him, not in the way this glint of amusement filled his eyes.

I heard a little chuckle from one of the men sitting on the couch, but I didn't look over. A survival instinct told me I needed to keep my gaze locked on the man currently advancing on Laura and me.

He stopped in front of Laura first, but I didn't miss how his focus kept flicking toward me. He didn't touch her, but then again, he didn't need to by how strong his gaze was as it moved up and down her body. Laura faced forward, her eyes locked on something straight ahead. It was very clear she had gone through this process before. Was this just something he did for every woman who worked here? It seemed so... wrong.

"Svetlana," he said as he stopped in front of Laura. He nodded to Boris, and Laura stepped back, her face a mask of indifference. Or maybe it was fear.

She put on a completely different persona at this place compared to Sal's. Then again, Sal's was like the juices at the bottom of a dumpster in comparison to this place.

He stepped close to me, and my body tensed involuntarily. The corner of his lips tipped up as if he found it funny... or it pleased him.

"What's your name, *dorogoy*?"

I felt light-headed, my heart racing so hard and fast I worried there was a possibility I'd pass out. I licked my lips and whispered, "Lina." He didn't show any facial expressions, just watched me with cold indifference.

"Do you know who I am?" His voice was thickly accented, yet the words were smooth and clear, his English flawless. I slowly shook my head, and that had a smile spreading across his mouth, but it wasn't the type of smile that put someone at ease. If a predator in the wild could grin, I knew this was what it would look like.

"It's always so thrilling when someone doesn't know who I am." The arrogance laced in his words terrified me. "It's Leonid, darling."

He didn't circle me like he had Laura, not at first. He stood just a foot away from me and stared, not speaking anymore, as if he'd made his quota for the day. The weight of his gaze was unsettling. I didn't know what he was looking for, or if he saw the answer to his own question, but after a second he started walking around me in the same process he had for Laura.

I could feel his gaze rake over each part of my body, as if his eyes were fingers and he was touching my calves, the backs of my thighs, my ass, and moving up the length of my spine. He was in front of me again, his focus on my chest, then lower. I stopped myself from covering my breasts and the junction between my legs, because even though I was fully dressed, I felt like this man could see right through the material.

"Svetlana?" one of the men on the couch asked.

He slowly shook his head. "*Net.*"

A string of Russian was spoken, the man before me holding my focus as if he knew who I truly was, as if he could see my deepest secrets.

He was like Arlo in that regard.

Dangerous.

"*Nevinovnyy.*" Leonid's voice was low and deep. But sharp... so sharp. "*Da,*" he said as if answering his own question. "Anastasia."

I opened my mouth to ask what was going on, but Laura took my hand and led me out of the room and back to where the other women and racks of clothing were.

"What's going on?" I finally asked when we stopped, and she faced me. "That was the weirdest damn interview, or whatever the hell that was, I've ever experienced. Who was that man?"

"Leonid Petrov," she said, but I didn't miss the slight tension in her voice. "He owns the bar." Her shoulders relaxed. "And I'm sure a shitload of other places, and big connections, no doubt." She didn't emphasize what she meant, but I got the gist. Connections in the crime world. I glanced around, and I felt like the pressure that had surrounded us when we were in front of Leonid slowly dissipated the longer we were away from him. "Damn, I wish we had gotten the same room together, but we snagged the top two tiers, so good money regardless."

I just shook my head. "This is the weirdest night I've had in a long time."

She snorted, and we both grinned genuinely.

"It's confusing the first time," she finally said. "Each room is named after a woman."

I stifled my eye roll. *Of course they are.*

"I got Svetlana. You got Anastasia... which is the highest-level tier. It's the one where the most important clients stay. So, in all regards, you hit the motherload for the tip jackpot."

For a moment I thought about just saying never mind and leaving. This was all so weird, and I was definitely an outsider. The women around me speaking Russian and the elite atmosphere solidified that.

I opened my mouth to thank Laura for getting

me the job, but I changed my mind when the words froze in my throat as I saw a woman walk in. She held a stack of folded-up bills and proceeded to unroll them and count her very clear tip money.

Holy shit. There are hundred-dollar bills in there. I took a steadying breath and looked at Laura again. I could see by her expression she expected me to bail. *Only this one time. If I make enough, this night will be a game changer.*

"Okay. Let's do this." Even I could hear how hesitant I sounded.

10

Arlo

P etrov wants to meet you tonight at *Sdat'sya.*
Midnight. Sharp.

That was the text I'd gotten an hour ago, and as I
pulled my car to the side parking of *Sdat'sya*, I
checked the clock on the dashboard. Ten minutes
until midnight.

When Leonid wanted to meet you personally, it
was never a good thing. He always wanted something. Always tried to squeeze the last drop of blood
from your body before he tossed your corpse aside.

And I knew what this was about. I knew Leonid
was going to try to talk me into joining the Bratva
instead of being a free agent—a mercenary even—

with the Ruin. He'd tried before, but with men like him, they were never satisfied if they didn't get exactly what they wanted.

Leonid was one persistent bastard.

I made my way toward the front entrance, pulled the heavy black door open, and immediately heard the soft sounds of traditional Russian music playing overhead. There was a Bratva soldier situated in the corner of the room, his long leather jacket concealing the no doubt numerous guns and knives he had attached to his body underneath.

This front entrance room was nothing but the first layer of *Sdat'sya*. It was the makeup before you got to the meat and heart of what this establishment really was.

There was a bar across from me, a few of the clientele lounging on the dark brown leather couches situated around the room. The majority of the people were in the other rooms, each one blocked off from prying eyes and ears, all of them housing a powerful, influential, and wealthy clientele. This wasn't just a bar; it was a place where a lot of the Bratva and powerful associates and allies who worked for and with them made deals, talked business, and used the amenities the Desolation Bratva had in abundance.

Drugs, booze, and women.

Behind the red and blacklight illuminated bar was a saying a lot of Leonid Petrov's men lived by.

Мы грешим, так как бы беспечны и не думаем об этом

We sin because we're careless, and we don't think about it. Or so it was translated loosely into English. But the truth was, that was a lie. Anyone involved in our world knew what the fuck they were doing. They were aware of their "sins," ones they didn't even see as such because the fuckers got off on giving pain to others. Like me. Like anyone associated with the Ruin.

No one bothered me. No one tried to stop me. Some even looked at me with clear fear and hesitancy in their eyes. Anyone who worked at *Sdat'sya* was part of the Ruin and therefore knew exactly who *I* was. They'd seen me at Yama, watched me destroy my opponents. They knew my reputation... the fact that I was a father killer. I wore that badge of patricide like a fucking honor.

I passed the bar and made my way down the

hall. There was a Bratva soldier standing at the end by the elevator. He straightened from the wall and gave me a nod of acknowledgment. He said nothing as he hit the button for the elevator to go upstairs, and a second later the elevator doors opened.

I stepped inside, the soldier following me in. Once we were ascending, I sorted through what would happen tonight. The one other time I had personally spoken with Leonid was right after I'd killed my father. He wanted me to join the Bratva then. I'd professionally declined. He hadn't pressed it, but I knew men like him. I knew *him* specifically. The way he worked, the things he demanded. How he expected the world to fall at his feet. And for the most part, it did.

But I wasn't like most of the world. I'd never submit to any man.

Leonid Petrov was dangerous and violent. He was a sociopath who killed simply because it was Sunday or he'd just finished a family meal. And his two sons, Dmitry and Nikolai, followed perfectly in his footsteps. Baby psychopaths in the fucking making.

"He's in his office, waiting for you," the soldier said in Russian.

I headed toward Leonid's office, passing closed

doors that led to private rooms for his clientele. There was a soldier standing off to the side beside Leonid's office. He gave me a nod before turning to open the door for me.

I stepped inside and instantly took in the surroundings. You had to know the layout of any place to be prepared. I saw Dmitry and Nikolai sitting on the couch in front of the fire. Dmitry, eldest son to Leonid and heir to the Desolation Bratva underworld empire, watched me with the same sociopathic glint in his eyes I knew was reflected back from mine. I'd heard the stories of Dmitry, of his initiation, of how he'd slaughtered five men with brutal clarity and force that had even momentarily impressed me. He'd be the perfect Pakhan one day, no doubt, a leader who made Satan cower in the dark.

Nikolai, Petrov's youngest son, let a slow, sardonic grin spread across his face. He might have been the "lighter" of the two in terms of brutality, but his easygoing attitude and what others might see as "soft" was nothing but a twisted facade of a man who I knew had once torn off the finger- and toenails of a poor bastard who'd cut him off in traffic.

Nikolai didn't bother with the glass for his

alcohol and instead held up the whiskey bottle and tipped it in my direction in greeting before giving me a wink as he brought it to his lips and took a long drink.

Leonid was in the middle of a conversation on his cell phone. My shoulders tensed and my fingers twitched to go for my gun just being in the same room with the bastard.

Once he was off the phone, he leaned back and clasped his hands to rest them on top of his abdomen. He gave me a slow smile, one that was anything but pleasant. The fucker didn't know happiness, not if it didn't involve slitting someone's throat and bathing in their blood.

Dmitry and Nikolai started a conversation with each other, the Russian too low for me to hear. Leonid rose and walked around his desk before leaning against the edge and staring at me with dark, unflinching eyes.

"I wanted to personally thank you for handling the... little issue we had the other night with Maksim." Leonid's words had his sons' conversation stopping. Although I kept my gaze on the Pakhan, I sensed his sons standing and walking toward him before they flanked their father. Their expressions were the same stony composure as the leader of the Bratva.

"No thanks needed," I said, focusing on Leonid. The other two little shits not something I was afraid of. "It's what I do."

Leonid inclined his head in agreement. "You can't understand how hard it was for me not to just dispose of that trash myself." He took his hands out of his pocket and smoothed them over his tie, one that was silk and colored bloodred, the same shade that seeped out of the hundred different wounds on the man who'd offended Leonid. "But you see, it wouldn't look good for me in our business. We don't deal with that messy side of things." He grinned and held his hands out. "Bad for business, you understand. We need to keep up appearances."

I wasn't sure why he was telling me any of this. He'd taken a fucking melon baller to the poor fuck's eyes. His fingers had been cut off and part of his scalp torn from his skull. Not to mention the other twenty brutal acts I'd noticed covering his body. Or missing from it. And all because the bastard had *looked* at Leonid's eighteen-year-old daughter. His precious Tatiana.

Although Leonid and his sons could've been called psychotic, and that would've been an understatement, I was pretty sure the fucker who had his life ended pretty damn violently had probably done more than just *looked*.

The kind of death the man had gotten would have been because of an act of aggression toward her, an insult whispered in her direction, or even an obscene look. The fucker probably hit on Tatiana.

His dick had still been intact—or so I'd unfortunately noticed, since he'd been naked when I'd been dispatched to get rid of the body—so I knew he hadn't actually touched Tatiana. If the poor bastard had, they would've cut his cock off and shoved it in his mouth to make a point.

I waited for Leonid to say what else he wanted. The *real* reason he'd called me here tonight wasn't to give me personal thanks for the job I'd done.

"Come, have a drink with me."

Before I could've said anything—not that I would've declined the invitation, which would've been in bad form—Leonid and his sons were walking past me and out the door. I followed the pack out of his office, the soldier coming up behind me as we made our way toward one of the elite rooms. On the door, a beautiful script in Russian was written in gold leaf.

Анастасия. *Anastasia.*

The double doors swung open as if on their own, and I followed Leonid inside. He headed straight toward the bar that stretched along the entire back wall, the decor in Anastasia all black-lacquered and golden accents.

I noticed a drunk and boisterous man off to the side, his Bratva tattoos visible on his arms deeming him a high ranking member. His voice was slurred as he shouted in Russian at the sex workers who'd been brought in as entertainment. His words were crude and sexual, and it was clear by his heavy-handed intoxication that he was probably a violent drunk.

I curled my lip in disgust as he started manhandling one of the women, her high-pitched giggle practiced if not forced.

There were a handful of other Russian men in the room, their overly excited and loud voices, the illegal cigars they smoked, and the constantly filled glasses of liquor creating a dangerous, sloppy atmosphere. Too much groping, damn near fucking, and a lot of money being exchanged for "extras."

The furniture was set up in several loose circles of couches and chairs, men sitting on the leather with barely dressed women perched on their laps. An elaborate crystal chandelier hung from the center of the ceiling, prisms of light cutting across the room and giving an almost hazy quality to the surroundings.

A fire roared between two large, dark couches, the flickering, low light casting shadows but unable to hide the debauchery currently taking place. Women were starting to become half-dressed as their breasts were exposed, hands disappearing into laps and through open flies and unbuttoned slacks.

The smell of Cuban cigar smoke filled the air, the low, sexually laced female laughter sounding in my ears. When we were at the bar, I kept my body sideways so I could see the entire room and have the entrance in sight. I kept my right hand free in case I needed it to pull my gun out. And then I just stared at Leonid as he ordered four glasses of whiskey. As the drinks were being filled, Leonid gave me another sharklike grin, his teeth white and straight, his incisors a little too sharp.

"I was discussing with my sons the tension rising within the Bratva and Cosa Nostra, as well as with the 'Ndrangheta, who have just claimed territory in the west. Pressure is very high right now, many deaths as territories are being fought over."

I didn't say anything. The bartender slid the

drinks in front of us. I took mine, keeping my eyes on Leonid, and brought it to my mouth.

He grabbed his glass and tipped it in my direction before he brought it to his mouth and took a slow drink of the amber-colored liquid. I followed suit. His sons stood behind him like watchful shadows, their dark gazes locked on me as if they saw me as a threat. They were smart in that regard.

But I had no intentions of ending Leonid tonight, even if I thought he was a slimy fucker and the Bratva could do with a stronger Pakhan, one who was more rational and less psychotic.

As he'd said before... it would be bad for business.

"Because of the mounting violence," he said and set his glass down on the bar, his fingers staying wrapped around the crystal, "I'm going to need a powerful army behind me."

"The Bratva is stronger than ever," I replied.

"It is, but you and I both know how easily that can splinter before breaking irrevocably." He glanced around the room, but not once did I take my focus from him. "And you and I have a history, do we not?" He stared into my eyes once more.

I set my glass down then, the soft *clank* it made

on the polished wood seeming overly loud at that moment.

"You killing your father, a traitor among the Bratva, the same man who had been going behind our backs and selling information to the Italian mob, showed me how loyal you are, Arlo. I want you on our side fully. I need the most powerful at my back, the strongest men as my weapons." He held his hands out, palms up, his current grin slow and satisfied as if he were a cat who'd just caught the mouse. "Being a free agent doesn't and won't offer you the safety and stability the Bratva can."

"I don't need protection. I create my own." I noticed a slight tick under Leonid's smooth cheek because I pointed out the truth. "I like where I'm at, Pakhan. I don't wish to change anything." The shit my father had put me through, the fact that he'd killed Sasha, my mother, and the blood and bodies I'd had to wade through in order to reach the surface, wasn't anything I'd ever do again.

I got to a point in my life where I didn't have to work for anyone anymore. I worked for myself, had the Ruin as a conglomerate of other businesses I could choose from. My reputation and skill preceded me, and because of that, I didn't have to be tied down to one side. I could accept or turn down anything I wanted. I wouldn't get that with Leonid. He'd expect complete obedience and submission, no questions asked. A loyal dog.

And as I said those words, I could see on Leonid's face that the pleasant facade he'd put on was slipping. The sound of men shouting *"Na zdorovie"* before they drank filled the sudden silence. It did nothing for the tension that was now between Leonid and me.

And then his stoic expression cracked, and he smiled, but I wasn't a fool in thinking that he would just give up on trying to bring me on to his side fully. Because a man like him, a Bratva Pakhan, was used to getting his way in all things. And if that meant he had to steal, rape, or kill to get it, he was bastard enough to do it.

Several women came out from the back, black trays in their hands, each one topped with drinks. I didn't spare them much attention, just noticed the shift and change in the air. But then everything around me stilled as the last woman emerged, her white dress standing out among the red and black of the others, her long black hair piled high on her head, the elegant line of her neck and delicate length of her spine in full view.

Every muscle in my body tightened to the point

it was uncomfortable and hard to hide. This was the last place I'd ever expect to see Lina, the last place I'd ever want her to be. And when Leonid turned his attention to see what I was looking at, I knew I'd made a big fucking mistake. An interested and curious gleam entered his eyes as he noticed Lina and then slowly looked back at me.

"Gorgeous, isn't she?" he murmured in Russian, and the way he said those words told me he'd been undressing her with his eyes.

I curled one of my hands into a tight fist, my other hand flexing and relaxing with the need to draw my gun and place the end right between his fucking eyes, demanding he look away from her. He had no right to look at Lina, not when I knew all the depraved shit he was into, not when I also knew he dealt with human trafficking.

"Do you know her?" The tone of his voice told me he already knew the answer to that. I didn't bother responding. "She's got this innocence about her, one that just makes you want to do the filthiest things..." He murmured the last part, and his fucking sons chuckled.

If I'd wanted to, I could've drawn my weapon and shot all three of them before any of the other people in this room could have stopped me. Of course, I would've been shot dead right afterward, but at least Leonid and his little bastard sons would be in the ground with me.

He turned to look at me, a shit-eating grin on his face. I hated that he'd seen any kind of reaction in me, because men like him would use it to their advantage. They'd see it as a weakness. And I couldn't lie and say he was wrong.

Lina was a weakness, an addiction, and I hadn't even sampled. She made all rational thoughts leave my head, and she didn't even have to be in the same room to succeed.

Everything else faded away as I watched Lina start handing out drinks. I could feel Leonid's gaze on me, could envision the bastard smirking, as if he'd just found a chink in my carefully placed armor.

She hadn't noticed me yet as she walked around. The men eyed her like she was a piece of meat, slipping her money, leaning forward and whispering things that made her blush but also had her eyes narrowing.

She set a drink beside an old fuck, his smile wide and lewd as he ignored the half-naked woman on his lap, her breasts close enough to his mouth he could have licked them. He held out a fifty-dollar bill, a wink being added to the mix, and when she took it with a soft smile, I could see his other hand snaking out like he planned on palming her ass.

I curled my hand so tight into a fist that my nails dug into my flesh, opening up the skin, the pain feeling good. She stepped out of the way before he could touch her. The lucky bastard had just missed me mangling the appendage for daring to put his filthy fucking hands on her.

But I should fuck him up just for *thinking* he could touch Lina.

She fluttered around the room like a delicate hummingbird, and the entire time, all male eyes were latched on to her, as if they could smell the innocence pouring off Lina and wanted to destroy it. I understood perfectly why Leonid had picked this room for her. These men were the most powerful, the wealthiest... the ones who would pay a small fortune if a woman's virginity was up for auction.

This was also the only room Leonid came to.

I forced myself to look at him, seeing he already had a calculating expression on his face as he watched me. He saw too much, knew too much just by my reaction. And it didn't matter how much I tried—and would fail—to hide what I felt toward Lina. The fucker saw all. A man didn't become

Pakhan if he didn't know how to manipulate and control... if he couldn't look at someone and see their whole story flash in front of his eyes.

And then he broke the stare and looked to the side. I followed his line of vision and watched Lina move up to the overly drunken man who stood in the corner, the one who was too handsy with the girls. The one I knew was a violent drunk just by how he carried himself. I didn't know him, but if he was in this room, he was either very powerful or was closely connected to Leonid.

I didn't miss how she eyed the drunk almost warily, her instincts telling her he wasn't a good man. He was dangerous. She handed him his glass of liquor. His eyes were hooded and glossy as he stared down at her. He was a big asshole, broad shoulders and tall. Barely any neck. He had a light sheen of sweat covering his forehead, his red-rimmed eyes zeroing in on Lina, taking in her white dress, tracing the few strands of wispy hair that framed her face.

I could imagine the scent of alcohol that came through his pores. I felt Leonid look back at me, but I couldn't take my focus off the scene in front of me. Everything else faded even more until I had tunnel vision, until everything slowed. The bastard set his drink down, and just as Lina turned to leave, he wrapped his hands around her waist, pulling her forcibly back toward him so hard the tray she carried tipped out of her hands and fell to the floor, the glass that had sat atop it hitting the ground, the cup breaking and mixing with the spilled liquor.

I saw red as he slowly slid his hands up, his fingers right under her breasts. She pulled away forcibly enough that she stumbled a step forward. And then he groped her ass. I didn't realize I had been moving until I was right in front of him. He turned his attention to me, his dark, thick eyebrows pulling low, as if he were fucking pissed I'd dared to interrupt what he was doing.

His mouth was moving, and I could assume he was asking me what the fuck I wanted, maybe threatening to kill me. Without taking my gaze off him, I reached out and pulled Lina away from him, could feel her looking at me, could've assumed her eyes were wide and an expression of shock covered her face.

The fucker's mouth was still moving, faster now, his anger coating his face in a red hue, his eyes narrowing, a vein popping out in his forehead from his rage.

I was aware of words spilling from my mouth

and directed toward Lina. Words that would have been close to "Stay close to me. Everything will be okay." But my mind was too hazy with anger and possessiveness to grasp any kind of sanity right now or to make sure I'd even said the words out loud.

And then I felt a heavy weight in my hand—one of the decorative granite balls that sat on a few of the tables, the design reminiscent of the detailed work on Fabergé eggs.

I felt this low-level hum fill me as everything else blurred. I slammed the granite ball against the side of the fucker's head, and when he stumbled back, blood making a trail down his temple from the crack to his skull, I grabbed his wrist, slammed it against the wall, and twisted his arm so his palm was flush with the golden-threaded damask wallpaper. I brought the stone down on the center of his hand so hard I could hear the crack of bone splintering under the force and pushing through the buzz in my head. I slammed it on his hand again and again until all I saw was blood and broken bone, until all I tasted was the coppery tang coating my tongue, until I felt the warmth on my neck and covering my hands.

His mouth was wide, and I could imagine he was screaming right now, but I only heard the rush in my ears. I felt people closing in, but no one touched me, no one stopped me.

I let go of his hand, and he went to grab it with his uninjured one, maybe to cradle the gnarled appendage to his chest. I stopped him by grabbing his thick wrist and proceeded to do the same to that one, using so much force the bone became nothing but splinters and powder.

I let go of him and took a step back, letting the granite ball fall from my grasp. I felt the vibrations travel from my feet up my legs from the impact of it hitting the floor. The bastard fell to his knees and kept his arms close to his chest, his hands unrecognizable for how badly I'd destroyed them.

Now the fucker couldn't touch any female.

He can't touch what's mine.

I found myself looking at Lina, that powerful, heady buzz moving through my body, a high I always felt when the violence took over. She stood beside me with shock reflected on her face. Eyes huge, more white than blue and black. Pink lips parted. Skin so pale she looked like a porcelain doll.

I reached out and smoothed my thumb along her cheek, wiping away the splatter of blood that marred her perfect skin after I broke the fucker's hands. For her. That blood smeared along her cheek, like a beautifully violent stroke of a brush.

I hadn't admitted it before, hadn't let it really grow inside me until this very moment, but as I stared into Lina's horrified eyes, I knew without a doubt I'd burn Desolation—the entire fucking world —if it meant having her as mine.

Because I'd never let her go, and the look in her eyes told me she realized it too.

11

Galina

"*Dasvidaniya.*"

That one word replayed over and over again in my head, the word Leonid had said low and mockingly in that thick Russian accent. And he'd watched me the whole time as Arlo led me out of the bar.

I now sat in the passenger seat of a Mercedes that had been parked at the side of the building. My heart was racing so fast and hard that my pulse was a constant *thump-thump* in my ears. I stared down at my backpack, not knowing how it was sitting on my lap, not knowing who had gotten it. I'd had it with me when I entered, my clothes stuffed inside when I changed, and as I curled my fingers around the old, stained nylon, all I saw was blood and gore and violence.

"You've put Dima out of commission," Leonid had said with controlled amusement. *"You'll owe me, Arlo. I'll call, and you'll come. Remember, I now know your weakness."* He'd said that last part while his gaze locked on me.

"What did he mean?" My voice was surprisingly strong given the fact that I felt as if I was having an out-of-body experience. I wasn't a stranger to violence. It was all brutal. But what I'd witnessed from Arlo, the way he used that decorative stone ball... it had been unlike anything I'd ever seen before.

He looked completely in his element, calm as he brought it down on that man's hands over and over again with bone-crushing force and precision. And his face... God, his face had been so void of *anything*.

My breath caught in my throat as I kept replaying those images over and over again. And he'd done it because that man had touched me. I knew that as well as I knew I was sitting in his car, letting him take me somewhere unknown.

I hadn't even put up a fight as he pulled me out of the bar, as he opened the door and all but set me on the leather seat of this car. I let him buckle the seat belt around me, his scent spicy and masculine with dark undertones that filled my nose, washing away the coppery scent of blood that had consumed my senses up until that point.

He didn't speak, but he didn't have to, to tell me the answers I needed. I could look at him and know exactly the type of man he was, who he was down to his very soul.

A killer.

Aside from the subtle tightening of his fingers on the steering wheel, his expression was closed off.

I stared at his hands, covered with now-dried blood. I wanted to ask him again what Leonid had meant, even though I could put two and two together. I would have had to be blind to not see that Leonid and Arlo were one and the same. Even worse than the men I'd grown up around in Vegas.

Then why am I not afraid of Arlo? Why do I feel like he'd kill a man to protect me... that he almost did?

"Where are you taking me?"

He stayed silent for so long that I assumed he wouldn't answer.

"My apartment," he finally said, and my heart jackknifed in my chest.

Something deep and dark in my body came

alive. He cut me a quick glance before focusing on the street again, his fingers tightening once more on the steering wheel.

"If I wanted to hurt you, I wouldn't have to take you to my apartment to do it." He stated those words so matter-of-factly it was like he'd read my mind. "You're safe." A long moment passed before he said so low I almost didn't hear, "Even from me."

Twenty minutes later we were outside the city limits of Desolation and pulling into an underground garage. He parked, climbed out, and walked around the front to open the passenger door before I could do it myself. For a second I just stared up at him, my breath stalling at the cold, detached look on his face.

"Come on, Lina." His tone was hard and sharp. It was dangerous.

I slipped my hand in his and repressed a shiver, but I didn't know if it was one of disgust because of what I'd seen him do, or because I liked the feel of his slightly callused hand wrapping tightly around mine and helping me out of his car.

I followed him toward an elevator, and he passed a silver key card across a sensor. The doors opened immediately. And then we were enclosed together as it ascended.

I should have been freaking out. I should have been demanding he take me to my apartment. I shouldn't have been staring down at my hands as I curled them even tighter around the straps of my backpack and watched them shake. I shouldn't have kept my mouth shut and let my gaze trail over my dress that I now noticed was covered in pin-sized dark spots.

Blood... blood covered me.

I didn't know anything about Arlo except for his name and what he ate at the diner every time he came in. His expression was always so stone-cold, as if he was so untouchable by everything and everyone that he couldn't bother to care. And as I glanced at him, his profile severe and cut in masculine lines and strong features, I couldn't find the words to say anything. I couldn't find my voice to tell him to take me back to my apartment, even though that was the last place I wanted to go. *Because I don't want to be alone.*

I was rattled and shaken, not sure what the hell just happened. He'd beat a man, pulverized his hands, all because of what? The man had groped me, yeah, but Arlo had acted out of such rage I was having a hard time breathing now just thinking about it.

Maybe all of this was some personal vendetta between the two men, because surely I would have no bearing on what Arlo did or didn't do. Before my thoughts could get even more tangled, the elevator stopped, and the doors opened. He stepped out first, and for a moment I just stood there, unsure if I should follow.

A part of me felt like I was stepping through the gates of hell itself. But I found myself moving on my own accord, the elevator closing silently behind me. I smelled lemon cleaning products right away, and with the lights completely off, the only things I could make out were what the city lights touched coming through the massive windows.

Oh. Wow.

My gaze was riveted to those windows, ones that took up one entire wall of his apartment, the city and sky stretching out for as far as you could see. It looked like it could have been cut from a postcard, how perfect it all seemed, how clean and docile... so not dangerous.

I focused on Arlo again, telling myself I probably shouldn't turn my attention from him. With the shadows and light that shone through the large windows making up one entire wall, I could make out certain parts of his home. Large couch to the left. A massive TV on the wall across from the furniture. The kitchen was to the right, all dark, smooth counters and sleek stainless-steel appliances.

I expected him to turn my way, to say something now that we were in his domain, but he still said nothing, just walked ahead of me, the soft sound of his shoes hitting the floor seeming louder than it probably should.

"Are you okay?" I finally asked, although it felt so stupid to ask a question like that.

He braced his hands on the bar and hung his head for a second before he let out a low, short, humorless laugh. "You're the one who was sexually assaulted tonight, and you're asking *me* if I'm okay?" He turned just his head so he could look at me, the shadows from the dark apartment and figments of light coming through all the windows from the city right behind the glass making him seem almost sinister.

"Yeah. I guess I am." We stared at each other for so long it started to become uncomfortable. My body shouldn't be feeling hot, so hot that I felt a trickle of sweat trail down between my breasts.

His eyes were hard, dark. Intense. "You're in shock."

Maybe I was. But I had never felt as clearheaded as I did right now.

And me feeling like I was burning alive had nothing to do with the temperature and everything to do with the man standing just feet from me.

"Why did you bring me here?" I was fidgeting as I ran my hands up and down my thighs, picked at an invisible thread at the hem of the dress, and kept shifting on my feet, the *clack-clack* of my heels sounding deafening.

He didn't respond as he turned and poured himself a drink. He held his arm out and tipped the bottle in my direction, and I found myself nodding before clearing my throat and asking him for a drink too, even though alcohol was the last thing I needed right now.

Once the glass was filled, he turned and walked back to me, holding it out, our fingers brushing as I took it with a shaky hand. I didn't miss how his eyes tracked the movement as I tightened my fingers around the smoothness of the glass in hopes I could gather my control. He didn't stop following my movements with his eyes as I brought the rim to my mouth and took a long drink.

That numbness faded and the fear and anxiety coursed through me so forcefully I drowned in the liquor, inhaling it without realizing, the acidic burn of it settling in my belly like a stone in the pit of my stomach.

He didn't show any emotion as he brought his own vodka to his mouth and took a long, slow drink. He swallowed it so smoothly it could have been water for all I knew. Then he turned and headed to the bar for a refill.

The silence stretched on, the loudest thing I'd ever heard. I stood there in the center of his lavish, expensive apartment, holding a glass of vodka and wearing another man's blood on me like an accessory.

"I brought you here because it's the only place they can't touch you. It's the only place you're truly safe right now."

His words had my heart lodging in my throat. I said nothing as I finished off my alcohol, the burn already making a warm, pleasure-numbing path through my veins, my eyes watering, but I blinked it back before the tears slid down my cheeks.

He turned around to face me, drinking his second glass and watching me over the rim.

"Why would they want to hurt me?" My voice was too low, too thin. I was terrified, not just about what had happened back at that bar—with that man —but what Leonid had meant by his parting words.

Your weakness.

But most of all, the most suffocating reason why I was terrified was because as I stood across from Arlo, all I felt was the need to go to him, to press my body against his and let our darknesses coexist.

"Why would I be on a man like that's radar?" Those words were whispered, and still Arlo didn't speak even though I knew he heard me. But I didn't need him to say the words to know the answer to the question I asked. Yet again I kept firing them at him, now more than ever wanting him to lie—to deny— what I said, what I felt.

"It's my fault," he finally said, but there was no guilt in his voice. There was... nothing. He tipped back his glass to finish off his vodka before setting it on the bar behind him. "I shouldn't have let him see my reaction." The last part was said almost as if he spoke to himself.

"I don't know what the hell's going on," I admitted softly before finishing off my liquor as well. I coughed, covering my mouth with the back of my hand as the burn settled in deep. It was fire down my throat and coalescing in my belly. It was a lightheadedness that made the situation a little less dreadful.

I turned from Arlo and walked toward the windows, the glass starting at the floor and going all the way to the ceiling foot after foot above me, nothing but skyscrapers and twinkling lights as far as the eye could see. Down below, there was nothing but red and white lights moving back and forth. Did the people there know the world they lived in? Did they know the evil men behind the designer suits and gentle smiles? Did they know death was right in front of them, and they opened their arms to embrace it like a warm friend?

I could see Arlo coming to stand behind me in the reflection of the glass, but I couldn't find it in me to feel any kind of fear. And although there was this awareness inside me that this man was dangerous, I never felt that his violence or aggression would ever be directed toward me. It was illogical. It was fucking stupid.

I knew nothing about Arlo, but if I looked hard enough, I could see his entire story written right on the surface.

"You're a bad man," I said as I stared at his reflection. He was looking down at me, his dark brows pulled low. He lifted a hand and ran it over his mouth, the sound of his palm moving over the stubble that created a light shadow across his cheeks and jaw loud right beside my ear. It was masculine. Arousing. It shouldn't have turned me on, but it did.

"I am." That word was final. So final that I felt a chill race up my spine as he said it in that low voice.

"Are there worse men out there than you?" I didn't know why I asked the question. Because truthfully I knew the answer.

"No."

I wanted to say I didn't believe him, but I'd be lying to both of us.

"But there are men out there who would hurt you, Lina... simply because you're associated with someone." I knew he meant associated with *him*. "They'd hurt you to make a point, to take a perceived weakness and snuff it out." His gaze was so fierce.

My heart hiccupped. Was he saying *I* was his weakness? I didn't even know him. How could I control someone *that* much? But my words were thrown back at me because the feelings I had when I was in Arlo's presence were soul-searing.

What Arlo unknowingly made me feel was hot enough to burn the wings off an angel.

My breath caught at the cold calculation, what he implied. *What he's saying.*

"And it's taking every single ounce of self-control I don't even possess not to go back there and kill any bastard who would take your life as if it meant nothing."

I didn't know why I turned around, didn't know why I faced the predator head-on. But as he took my now-empty glass from my hand and set it aside, his eyes never leaving me, there was nothing on this earth that could have forced me to look away.

I moved my arms behind me and pressed my palms flat against the window. The glass was cold and smooth beneath them. Hard. I curled my fingers against it, even though I knew it wouldn't give me any purchase.

I stared into his eyes that looked so dark with the shadows gently caressing him like a lover. And I knew the absolute truth the longer he stared at me, peeling away bit by bit, exposing me inch by inch.

"Did you kill that man in the alley?" I knew I wouldn't have to specify what and who I meant.

One.

Two.

Three seconds passed before he moved in an inch closer. "Yes."

He said that word as if it was the easiest thing to admit. As if killing was the simplest form of pleasure. I held my breath, his truth like a sledge-hammer to my chest.

"Ask me why I did it." Low voice. Deep words. Tearing me from the inside out.

"Why did you kill him?" There was a hitch in my voice that I knew couldn't go unnoticed.

He leaned in until his lips were close enough to my ear that his answer would brush along the shell. "For you."

My heart was running a race in my chest. *Bu-bump. Bu-bump.* "What are you?"

His smile was slow. Evil. He moved a step back, and I sucked in a breath.

"I told you." One. Two. Three seconds. "The bad guy."

12

Arlo

I didn't want to frighten her. I wanted to pull her against my body and hold her head to my chest, tangle my fingers in the long fall of her hair, and whisper all the words that would let her know how safe she was.

I wanted to know everything about her. I wanted her to *trust* me.

She hid things about her life, her past, present, and future. I wanted to tear those secrets away until she was just as vulnerable to me as she'd made me to her. I didn't even know how or why or fucking *when* it happened, but this woman had changed something monumental in my life. I hated it.

I couldn't live without it.

Months. It had only taken a moment to look into her innocent eyes to know there was something light and different the world could offer... something that could *shape* me. Only a handful of months to turn my world upside down without her even having to utter a word.

A. Fucking. Look. That's all it took to go down this rabbit hole where, for the first time in my miserable life, I questioned my very sanity. *For the first time in my life, I want something just for* me.

And as I stared into her blue eyes that looked so dark right now, not because of the shadows or lack of light but because she was vulnerable in my presence, I told myself there was no going back.

I'd lost it in front of Leonid, showed him a weakness in his own fucking house. He wouldn't forget it. He'd use it against me. He'd twist it and use it to his advantage. It's what men like him did. It's what I did.

I'd seen it in the way he looked at me when I took Lina out of there. When he stared at *her*.

I turned away and stalked back to the bar, pouring myself more vodka. Too much. I tossed it back and went for glass number four. The burn wasn't there any longer, and alcohol was the last thing I needed. My head was already fucked up without the temptation of Lina in my apartment and the cloudiness of booze in my veins.

I shouldn't have told her I killed that fucker in the alley. But I'd taunted her, needed her to ask me so I could *show* her how far a man like me was willing to go for *her*.

"Who are you? Who are those men? What is actually going on?"

I didn't turn around to face her. I stared at the wall straight ahead, my glass in hand, my fingers tight enough around the glass I hoped it cracked and tore my hand to shreds. It would give me something else to feel.

"I'm a ba—"

"I know. You're a bad man. I didn't ask what people see when they look at you, not what you see in the mirror. I want to know what's going on, because if what you say is true—"

"It is," I said, cutting her off.

"Then with my life in danger, you owe me the truth."

How could this woman utter a few words and have something tight and uncomfortable inside my chest and squeezing my vital organs? I was now regretting not looking into her past, not getting any and all information on Lina that I could. I didn't have a moral compass, yet when it came to her and finding out who exactly Lina Michaels was—who she *really* was—I found myself holding back, wanting her to be the one to confide in me.

It was fucking stupid. A mistake. I ran a hand over my face.

I turned around and looked at her. She was still against the window, but her gaze was steady as she watched me. It would be so easy to go up to her and press our bodies flush together, to curl my fingers around her throat and make her look into my eyes as I tell her she's mine.

Fuck, I envisioned myself burying my face in her hair and inhaling deeply before running my nose down the length of her throat, dragging my tongue up and down her soft skin. I could practically taste her in my mouth. Sweet. So sweet. I wanted to feel how fast her pulse would beat against my tongue, proving that she was just as affected by me as I was by her.

"Don't ask questions you don't really want to know the answers to." Did she want me to admit I was involved in the crime syndicate? Did she want to know everything that touched me, everything I owned, was because of blood money?

She pushed away from the window and took a

step toward me, but I didn't miss the tremor that moved through her body. She was trying to be stronger than she felt. It was an admirable quality, but it was also a weak one. A human one that would do her no good.

Lina kept moving closer, watching me cautiously. How close would she come? Would she get so close I could reach out and curl my fingers around her waist? Close enough to where I could press her body to mine and let her *feel* the physical reaction she brought out of me?

"Are you part of that...?" She didn't finish that question, but she didn't need to. She knew what I'd say if I could have. She just wanted me to verify it. I couldn't. I wouldn't. It wasn't even about some moral compass, wasn't because of the Bratva or the Cosa Nostra. At this point I didn't care about any of that. I'd never tell her, because it would put her in even more danger.

I said nothing. There were no words I could say. She looked away when it was very clear she understood, when she knew she wouldn't get the answers she sought from me. I finished off my vodka and set the glass down. I tried to shut off my emotions, what I felt. They were messy and didn't do anything but cause issues. They made a conscience rise up in somebody like me.

"So what?" She looked back at me. "You can't take me home because I'm in some kind of danger now?" She scoffed and looked away. *So brave. Trying to be so strong.* It was a turn-on. "You know nothing about me." She looked back at me then, trying to hide the fear in her eyes.

But it wasn't for me. She was afraid of something else. Her past. I wanted to find who'd hurt her, who'd betrayed her, and make them beg me for death.

"I've known bad men my whole life. I know how to survive. I don't need anyone protecting me."

Something dark and possessive unfurled in my chest, tightening my heart, causing it to grow, the organ pulsing so hard I was sure it would rip through and crack my ribs.

I wanted to be the one to protect her. I wanted to be the one who killed anything that threatened her.

"Why are you doing this?" she whispered, and I hated that she had a tremor in her voice.

You know why. Or maybe you don't. But you will, and you'll be even more afraid of me, because you'll see I won't let you go.

But I didn't say any of that. I took a step closer and

watched her body tense, her eyes flare. "I caused issues for you with people you don't want issues with." I held her gaze with mine. "And until I fix it, until I can make sure you're safe, you'll stay here." She opened her mouth, most likely to protest, but a slow shake of my head and a thinning of my lips stopped her. "You'll stay here." I took a step closer. I wasn't lying about Leonid or the danger he presented, but I also wasn't being honest about the situation. I wanted her here for totally selfish reasons.

"You know nothing about me," she whispered again. I didn't answer. "My work. My apartment." She looked away.

"The apartment is a shithole."

She snapped her head in my direction and narrowed her eyes. Her annoyance was an accelerant to my lust. "That may be, but it's where I live," she said in a low voice, all but sneering the words at me. "And I need to work. I need the money." The way she clamped her jaw told me needing the money wasn't just about needing to keep that shithole of an apartment. She needed money for other reasons.

I said nothing as I stared into her eyes. I took a step closer until our chests almost brushed. I had to admit I fucking got off on the fact that she didn't retreat, that she held her ground and met my stare with a thinly veiled pissed-off one.

"Whatever you need, I'll provide."

She shook her head. "I don't like being indebted to anyone."

"Non-fucking-negotiable." I crossed my arms over my chest, knowing she had a hell of a lot more to say. "Besides, as stubborn as you are, you don't seem like the self-sacrificing type of human. Pretty sure you want to live, isn't that right?"

She pursed her lips even more. "And if I left when you're not here? Ran... from you?" There was this challenge in her voice that had my blood turning to fire. I let a dangerous smile cover my lips.

"I'd find you. No matter where you went." I closed off any emotion then, turned, and started walking toward the hallway. "I'll show you where you can sleep." I knew she'd follow. She was strong, but she wasn't stupid. Lina had felt the danger where Leonid was concerned, and although she knew I wasn't any better than the bastard, the unhinged aura Leonid didn't even try to conceal was too strong for her to ignore. And for whatever fucking reason, little Lina trusted me more than she trusted herself to stay safe.

She should fear me just as much as Leonid from

principle alone. But she didn't, and that had that possessive glint in me where she was concerned growing tenfold. One day it would consume both of us.

One day soon.

13

Galina

I stood in the center of what was clearly a guest room. I was pretty sure no one had ever even been in this room aside from a housekeeper. It was empty of life. It could have been a hotel room for how "warm and welcoming" it was.

I scanned the room and took in how sparse everything was. The queen-size bed pressed against the wall in the center of the room. One dresser across from that. A TV sitting on top of it. There was a padded chair beside the lone window, the sheer curtains in place allowing muted light to filter through. There was a small bathroom attached to the room, and one small landscape painting that hung on the wall beside the bed.

I walked up to the picture and stood in front of it. I hadn't bothered turning on the lights. I was already sucked into the darkness, so I might as well get used to it. I stared at that picture, a serene beach scene with tall grass frozen in a swaying motion from the wind, waves hitting against the shore and causing white peaks, a long stretch of sandy land leading to paradise. There was even a little bridge leading down to the water.

It was generic, probably had come with the apartment.

I turned and looked at my backpack that sat on the dark comforter in the center of the mattress. I walked over to it at the same time I got out of the dress, feeling like the material was permanently stuck to me because of the blood. I let it drop to the floor unceremoniously as I reached into my backpack and pulled out a T-shirt and a pair of shorts.

Once I was in the bathroom, I wasn't surprised to see a toothbrush and toothpaste, soap, shampoo, even face wash sitting on the counter. All unused. I could've imagined this was a swanky hotel stay if I wasn't being kept here against my will. But I wasn't stupid. I knew that man—Leonid—was bad. Very bad. And for whatever reason, Arlo wanted to protect me. I wasn't anybody special, had nothing to offer, but I wasn't going to look a gift horse in the mouth in my situation.

I couldn't pay him for keeping me safe. I could barely even afford to keep myself alive and safe from the men I was running from. I set my outfit on the granite bathroom counter and braced my hands on the edge, closing my eyes and just breathing. I didn't want to look at my reflection. I didn't want to see blood on my skin, a reminder of tonight.

So instead I ignored the mirror and grabbed the shampoo and body wash, went into the shower, and cranked it on as hot as I could stand it.

I scrubbed myself for twenty minutes until my skin was raw and red, until it was numb, and washed away any remnants of death. With my shirt and shorts on, I climbed into the bed, pulled the blanket over my head, and then let the darkness take me away.

SOMETHING LOUD WOKE me with a startle, my eyes surging open, my heart racing. I hadn't dreamed last night. I didn't see scary faces surrounding me in the darkness, didn't feel someone chasing me as I looked over my shoulder. I didn't dream of being held down and blood covering me. I couldn't remember the last time I'd slept so soundly, where the nightmares didn't drag me down and try to keep me there.

I pushed the blanket off my body and sat up, wincing from the kink in my neck from sleeping in the same position all night. Morning sunlight streamed through the window. Even though I knew the hectic-day life was in full gear just outside the glass and steel, I didn't hear honking cars or the thick life of traffic. I inhaled and smelled the faintest hint of lavender and lemon.

I heard another sound come from outside the room, and I stared at the closed bedroom door for a moment before forcing myself out of bed and into the bathroom. After I used the restroom, I brushed my teeth and washed my face. I looked at myself in the mirror. My long dark hair was in unruly waves and cascading down my shoulders and back, tangles touching my cheeks. My hair was even more crazy because I'd slept with it wet, and trying to tame it was a losing battle. I gave up, grabbed a hair tie from my backpack, and was back in front of the mirror, pulling the long fall off my shoulders and into a ponytail.

The bags under my eyes were horrendous, and they stood out like a neon sign against my too-pale face. But it didn't matter. I wasn't about to enter a beauty contest. I was quite literally trying to stay alive. So fuck it if I looked like the living dead.

I left the bathroom and shut off the light, headed toward the bedroom door, and gripped the handle, my nerves taking control. I opened the door and stepped out into the hallway but didn't move right away, just stood there trying to control my breathing. I didn't hear anything, just the stillness of the apartment, which was a little unnerving. But then I shook my head to clear it, feeling stupid. A quiet house should be the least unnerving thing going on in my life right now.

I stopped at the end of the hall and saw part of the kitchen and living room. My heart was thundering in my chest so loudly I wondered if it could be heard outside my body.

There was a light sound of something being set down, and I leaned to the side and looked into the kitchen. There, sitting at the small dining room table, was Arlo. My breath caught in my throat at the sight of him sitting there shirtless, tattoos covering his body, some that were very clearly Russian.

Bratva.

It all fell into place as I took in the stars on his shoulders, the Russian-style cathedral tattooed in vivid, gorgeous detail in the center of his chest, and a Russian nesting doll inked on his entire right side. He had a myriad of other dark and colorful ink along his broad shoulders, biceps, forearms, and very defined chest.

I felt a flush move through me so powerfully it was hard to catch my breath for a moment.

My gaze landed on the gun sitting right beside his hand on the dining room table.

Without looking up from the paper in front of him, he said in a deep, low voice, "If you're a coffee drinker, there's some in the pot. If not, all I have is water." He flipped a page on the paper. "The pastries were just delivered and are in a box on the counter."

I didn't move for a second, and he looked up at me, dark gaze slowly moving up and down my body. My shorts were high up on my thighs, my T-shirt long enough to cover them. It probably looked like I wore nothing underneath.

Although I was fully dressed, I couldn't help but feel like I was totally nude in front of him. I tugged on the hem of my shirt before diverting my gaze and making my way toward the kitchen. I could smell the coffee, and although I wasn't much of a fan, I figured now was as good a time as ever to get a little caffeine fix.

After I poured a cup, not bothering with sugar or milk because I didn't want to go rummaging through his things, I opened up the box and grabbed the first danish I could see. I could still feel Arlo looking at me, but I refused to meet his gaze.

Although I had so many more questions, I didn't know if he'd be forthcoming with the answers. But then again, I wouldn't know unless I asked.

After I swallowed a bite of danish and washed it down with some coffee, I set the cup on the granite counter and looked up at him. He was back to reading the paper, and from the distance I could see it was in another language—Eastern European if I had to guess by the letters.

Although he didn't have a noticeable accent, a few times I had heard a difference in the way he pronounced certain words. "I didn't realize you could get international papers in Desolation." Truth was, I didn't know if you could or couldn't get anything in this godforsaken city. I hadn't been here long enough, and it wasn't as if I'd checked out the lay of the land.

He leaned back in the chair, and I forced myself not to look at the way the muscles under his tattooed, golden skin flexed with that small movement.

Arlo was a big man, broad shoulders, a wide chest, and a ridiculously defined abdomen. I could see the gray sweatpants he wore from this vantage point, a very outlined V of cut muscle starting on either side of his waist and disappearing underneath the material. I picked up my glass and took a drink. As soon as I swallowed too much liquid, I regretted it.

I sputtered and wiped my mouth with the back of my hand, my eyes watering, my tongue burning because the coffee was so damn hot. I turned my back to Arlo and coughed a couple more times, patting my chest and only turned around once I could breathe again. He still had his focus on me, but the corner of his mouth was tipped up ever so slightly, as if he thought it was amusing. I found a spark of anger and annoyance moving through me, but I didn't say anything.

"Desolation can get anything you want, Lina." He lifted his coffee mug to his mouth and took a long, slow drink as he watched me. *Don't look at that bulging bicep. Don't watch the way it clenches and relaxes just from him picking up a damn ceramic mug.*

"Italian, Russian, Spanish. Any language you want... anything you want, you can get for a price." He set his mug down but kept his fingers curled around the handle. His other arm still rested over the back of the chair beside him. His position was easygoing and relaxed, and God, he made it look sexy.

Maybe I was suffering from some instantaneous Stockholm syndrome? But I knew that wasn't true. I'd felt this dark desire for him the moment I saw him months ago. Now that I was in his home... forced to stay here for my "own good," I felt like I was losing my mind slowly.

"Do you know how to fight?"

His question took me off guard, and I eyed him as I swallowed another bite of danish. "I think?" I felt my face heat at the stupid words that just spilled from my mouth. "Well, I've taken a couple self-defense classes and always carry pepper spray on me. I can defend myself if needed." I wondered if he'd seen me in the alley after I doused the asshole in the face with my pepper spray before kneeing him in the nuts and taking off.

Although the truth was, I'd gotten very lucky in that instance, in being able to leave. The bastard had been stronger, bigger. All it would've taken was my hands to be restrained and my bag tossed away, and I would've been at his mercy. I wasn't strong in the physical sense, and the few self-defense moves I knew wouldn't help me if somebody really wanted to hurt me.

"I'll teach you how to fight."

I felt my eyebrows rise to my hairline at his words. *Teach me how to fight?* It was on the tip of my tongue to tell him no, that fighting and violence were the last things I wanted. But was it really? I needed to learn to protect myself, not just from the Vegas shit, but all this other stuff now too.

"Nonnegotiable, Lina."

I didn't know if me defying him pissed him off or amused him. It was hard to read Arlo's expressions the majority of the time, because he kept himself so closed off.

"Okay," I said without any heat. I would've taken more of the self-defense classes in Vegas before fleeing, but funds and time hadn't really allowed it. And as I stared at him, I knew without a doubt Arlo could kill somebody with his bare hands if need be. "But can you tell me *why* you're doing this? Like, I understand the safety aspect, but why do you care? I'm a nobody."

He just looked at me, not speaking, but there was this hard tension around him. I knew I'd still get no answers from him.

Fine, if he wanted to give me a hard time, then I'd just show him how stubborn I was. "I need to work on my next shift." The hard set of his jaw told me he was about to argue, but I shook my head. "Listen," I said before he could go into whatever spiel he was about to say to me. "I don't know what mess I'm caught up in, because you won't tell me, but I know if you wanted to hurt me, I wouldn't be in your apartment right now, eating a strawberry danish and drinking bitter-ass coffee." His lips quirked slightly as if he was amused. "But I *have* to go to work. I can't just *not*. It's clear you're not hard up for money," I said and pointedly looked around his lavish penthouse apartment, "but I don't have that luxury or privilege. I..." I stopped before I could say I was running and needed all the funds I could get.

His eyes narrowed marginally when I wouldn't press on. It was very clear this man got what he wanted without anyone giving him shit about it, but I was already in a deep enough hole with my own problems, and then there was all this other stuff that was now laid in my lap. I just wanted to figure out how things were going to go and if they could even get better at this point.

But I wasn't ready to give up on this. If he wanted to "keep me safe" and force me to stay, then there was one thing he'd learn about me, and that was I didn't give up easily when I put my mind to something.

We were in this silent stare-off for a couple of seconds, and when he didn't speak, I exhaled and just pressed on. "I have to work," I said, softer this time, hating myself that I heard the defeat in my voice. "I know you said it's not safe, and I'm not stupid, but you don't understand, I *have* to make money."

"If you're in trouble, all you have to do is tell me and I can help." His voice was low and deep, but I didn't miss the edge, didn't miss the danger lying underneath.

"Maybe I don't want anyone's help." The words were so soft I didn't even know if he heard, but when he spoke, I knew he had.

"Maybe sometimes we have to ask for help, even if we don't want it."

I was shaking my head before he finished but couldn't find the words to say anything. I looked around his incredible apartment, took in the natural light filling the space, noticed all the expensive, sleek appliances, and didn't miss how everything screamed of wealth.

"You can't possibly know how it feels to struggle." I was assuming, and I shouldn't. I knew nothing about Arlo, where he came from or how he'd grown up. When I looked back at him, I could see the hardness back in his eyes.

"I had some clothing delivered for you."

He changed the subject so fast my head spun. He looked pointedly at my shirt and shorts. I didn't bother asking how he knew my size to order me anything. "You can't work out in those." He lifted his gaze back to my face. "We'll leave in an hour to teach you how to defend yourself, *moy svet.*"

I didn't know what he'd just said in Russian, but I could assume it was along the lines of "ungrateful bitch."

I exhaled and finished my danish and coffee, rinsed out my cup, and set it in the sink. I wanted to ask him over and over again why he was doing any of this, letting me stay in this posh apartment, feeding me, clothing me... protecting me. I just wanted to take his face in my hands and... kiss him.

Instead I picked up the bag he'd gestured toward

on the ground by the breakfast bar and walked away, mentally adding up how much I'd owe Arlo after this was all said and done.

And as I walked back to the guest room to change, I felt him watching me the whole time.

14

Galina

This felt like it was a *really* bad idea as I stood across from Arlo in a questionably stained—possibly once white—boxing ring.

We'd left almost two hours ago from his apartment. I'd taken in the wealthy part of the city, remembering the glittering skyscrapers that seemed to touch the heavens, where people walked up and down the streets without the fear of getting pulled into a dark alley.

I'd stared out the window of his car and saw the affluence slowly turned into that ugliness Desolation was so known for.

I didn't need to ask if this gym was Russian. That

had been clear when we stepped inside and I saw the massive Russian flag hanging behind the boxing ring, coupled with the fact that all I heard was men shouting and talking in another language.

At first, I'd had in this weird moment of awe as I followed Arlo inside, the gym bag hanging loosely from his strong, broad shoulders. Although all the noise sounded like there were a hundred men crammed inside, there was probably only a handful, all of them so big and loud it made my ears ring. But as soon as they noticed Arlo, the conversation stopped, all eyes on us.

He said something low but loud enough that it carried through the small interior. And then I watched in confusion and a little bit mesmerized as the men left. As in they *left* the gym.

I glanced around. The place appeared run-down, decades old. The boxing ring itself was battered, with dark tape holding some of the roping together that surrounded us, the white beneath my feet stained in brown, rusty shades.

I looked at Arlo again, the white T-shirt he wore hiding almost all the tattoos on his chest, yet I could make out the dark ink and shapes beneath the thin, light-colored material. "Is this place owned by the Russian mafia?" I had no idea why those words came from my mouth. I felt my eyes flare in surprise and a little bit of fear.

I didn't want to get on his bad side, although I didn't know if Arlo had a good side.

I also had no idea if blatantly talking about the Bratva would piss him off. Not that I knew anything about the former, but if I were to guess, I assumed this place was hard-core mafia territory.

"It's owned by Ivan." He smirked.

I licked my lips and started moving my hands up and down my thighs. "Ivan, huh?"

He nodded once. Slowly.

I said nothing else, just kept running my sweaty palms up and down my thighs. The workout clothes Arlo had gotten for me were nothing but a pair of black leggings, some ankle socks, tennis shoes, and a form-fitted short-sleeve shirt. I was completely covered, modest even, yet whenever Arlo looked at me, I always felt so naked.

"What did you say to everyone to get them all to leave the gym?" I figured that was a safe enough conversation switch, but when he slowly shook his head, I had a feeling this might have been another "nonnegotiable" situation.

"I told them," he finally said, "you weren't a

sideshow, so I politely informed them the gym was closed for a private lesson."

This dark tendril moved through me at his words, because I knew what they were. A lie.

I watched the way his gaze tracked up and down my body, how his eyes moved along my form, lingering on the long lines of my legs, moving back up to skate over the most intimate part of me that was totally covered, so it wasn't like he could see anything, yet I felt a whole lot of heat in that moment.

Then he moved his gaze up my flat belly, over the small mounds of my breasts, and finally looked into my face. My nipples hardened under the sports bra and thin Lycra of my shirt. I tried to control my breathing, but I knew I failed. How could a look make me *feel* like this?

"I have a feeling that's not what you said to them," I said with a hint of teasing in my voice.

"It's too bad you don't speak Russian," he said, deep and low. "Then you'd know if I was telling the truth."

He was infuriatingly stubborn, and it turned me on like nothing else.

"*Interesno, kak by vy otreagirovali, yesli by uznali, chto ya skazal im, chto pererezhu im glotku, yesli oni khotya by posmotryat na vas*." He spoke deep and low, his words flowing through and around me.

I had no clue what he had said, but for some reason it caused a shiver to consume my entire body. The smallest tilt of his lips showed me he *knew* what effect he had on me. "What did you say?"

He took a step closer, and one more until he was now circling me. "You should learn Russian, *moy svet*."

That was the second time he'd called me that, but I was too flustered to ask what it meant. "Maybe you could teach me?" I had no idea why or how the words came out of my mouth, but I didn't take them back. It was presumptuous to think this man would help me any more than he already was. But as he stopped in front of me and I tipped my head back to look into his too-dark eyes, I idly wondered how much he would give me.

Arlo was so tall. At five-foot seven, I wasn't exactly short, but standing in front of him, my head only reached his pectoral muscles. He was so tall, so big that he was easily twice my weight. He made me feel safer than I ever had before.

I refrained from shivering at the thought and wondering if he was this big... everywhere.

He reached out, and my body tightened, but his

finger just barely brushed my neck. "*Gorlo*," he said as he curled his fingers around my throat.

I blinked up at him, and a second later he twisted me around until my back was to his hard chest. His hand on my throat was firm, but he made sure not to cut off airflow.

"*Plecho*," he murmured, his voice right by my ear as he placed his other hand on my shoulder. He slid his fingers down my arm and curled them around my wrist. "*Zapyast'ye*." Arlo moved his fingers down to curl around my hand. "*Ruka*."

God, I was burning alive as I felt his entire body stay flush with mine, as I felt his hot touch skitter along what shouldn't be erogenous zones but very clearly were as I grew wet and needy. I could feel a moan burning up my throat, but in the next second he tightened his hold on me and jerked my arm behind my back. With the fingers of one hand wrapped around my throat and his other hand keeping my wrist to the small of my back, I felt trapped.

And then he was gone, my body tilting forward before I righted myself.

"It's a good thing I'm going to teach you to defend yourself, because in that moment I could have done whatever I wanted, Lina."

I turned around to stare at him, my face hot, which I hoped he took as embarrassment and not arousal. Because it totally was the latter. My breathing was so shallow and fast, yet he was completely composed. Any kind of idea that this man might be attracted to me and that's why he was helping went out the window as I remembered when he had his body pressed against mine. I hadn't felt any clear signs he'd been turned on. *Not like me.*

And that thought had even more heat rushing to my face with embarrassment.

"Come on, Lina. Show me what you learned."

A part of me—one I should burn to the ground if I was smart—wanted him to call me by my real name. *Just say Galina. Call me Galina as you touch me.*

My heart was racing a mile a minute as I stared at him. Arlo was massive, but wasn't that the point of self-defense, to take down somebody who was bigger than you, who was a threat? But my couple of measly classes wouldn't help me in this instance. I'd gotten lucky with the drunk in the alley. He'd been inebriated. I'd caught him off guard, and then I'd run like hell. There was no running from Arlo. We were caged within these boxing ropes, but I knew even if I got out, he'd still get me. He'd find me, catch me... do whatever he wanted.

"I don't want to hurt you." My words were low and almost laughable even to my own ears. And then he smiled slowly, the first full-blown one I'd seen him give me in my presence. I wondered if this was the first one he'd ever worn.

It was terrifying... and so attractive.

He curled his finger toward me in that universal sign for *come here*. My legs were like jelly, my hands shaking. I felt a drop of sweat slowly trail down my temple. I went back to those classes I'd taken, forcing myself to look at Arlo like he was the threat he was portraying to me right now... the threat he was to everyone else.

I charged after him, aiming for his legs to take him down, but I only got a few steps before he wrapped a thickly muscled arm around my waist and lifted me off the ground. I gasped with the sudden rush of air and shift of the ground beneath me, and then once again he had my back to his chest, his arms keeping mine pinned to my sides.

"Show me again," he said darkly against my ear and let go of me.

I stumbled forward and tried to catch my breath. I turned around again, not sure what the hell I was doing, yet trying to look for a weak spot. I went after him again, but this time I ducked when I saw the subtle tensing of his arm. I knew he was about to grab me again. I managed to kick my leg out and get him in the calf, but his leg was like cement, hard and unyielding.

He had me off the ground and spun around so fast I grew dizzy. And then my chest was pressed against the boxing ring rope, Arlo's massive body against mine, every inch of him burning me where he touched.

"You should get your money back if this is what they taught you." I could hear the teasing, annoyed note in his voice, and my own irritation rose.

"You're bigger than me, stronger." I turned my head to the side so I could look at him, but that was a foolish move, as it brought our mouths danger-ously close together. "I don't have my pepper spray, and I don't have the added benefit of fearing for my life and getting that kick of adrenaline."

My breath caught, my lungs tightening, when this dark, strange look covered his face.

"You *should* be afraid right now, *moy svet*." His words were low... deadly. "You should be more afraid of me than anything else in the dark." He leaned in an inch. "If you knew who I truly was, you wouldn't be so close to me."

I looked down at where his hand gripped the

rope on either side of me, the tattoos on his fingers sneaking up the back of his hand disappearing and going up his wrist and forearm. I'd never been one to think tattoos were attractive, but on Arlo, it made him brutally beautiful to me.

"You're so tiny, *moy svet*." He made a low, gruff sound and pushed away from me. I closed my eyes and breathed out just as he said, "Again."

And so for the next several hours, I sparred and grappled with Arlo until I was sweaty and sore, more tired than I'd ever been, but had never felt more liberated in all my life.

15

Galina

The following day, the routine was the same. But I'd called off from my shift, knowing it was the smart thing to do even if it felt wrong with my end goal.

We ate breakfast before Arlo took me to the gym, where he barked out in Russian at the men there, which had them scattering out of sight, and then he proceeded to help me train for a few hours.

After a light lunch, we came back to his apartment, where I showered, then proceeded to pass out until dinner. My body ached, even my skin hurting from the almost brutal way Arlo had pushed me with self-defense.

And although I'd never been so tired before, I'd also never felt stronger or more sure of protecting myself. I'd never felt so... safe.

The sun had set an hour ago, and Arlo ordered Italian, which had just been delivered. The bags were fancy and black, gold lettering stamped across the front. I'd never eaten from anywhere that had delivery bags as swanky as these or, hell, delivery bags at all.

I was doing everything in my power not to look at him. I felt his eyes on me, so magnetic that I was hyperaware of every little move he made.

He hadn't gone to work—or whatever he did to make a living—since he'd brought me to his apartment, and my curiosity was starting to get the better of me, but I refrained from asking. I did have tonight off but was scheduled for Sal's tomorrow, and I wasn't going to miss it. No matter what he said.

I brought my fork to the chicken parm on my plate and cut off a piece, focusing way too damn hard on it. It was either that or look at Arlo.

The flavors burst in my mouth, the sauce rich and everything combining together as if the cook had been creating a masterpiece. But instead of his tools being a canvas and paints, he used tomatoes, basil, and other seasoning.

And it was the fact that I was trying so hard *not* to focus on Arlo, who sat across from me yet felt so close, that I was comparing food with painting.

For fuck's sake.

The tension in my body got too tight, but I finally looked up at him. He was leaning back and his body shifted to the side slightly, a glass in his hand with clear liquid filling it, liquid I knew wasn't water. He had one arm bent at the elbow and resting over the back of his chair, his focus trained on me. I actually shivered. I had no idea why this man had this kind of effect on me, but there was no pushing it aside.

There was no ignoring it or trying to act like I had a handle on anything. I didn't. My life was so messed up at the moment that any kind of relationship, including the sexual kind, shouldn't have even been a blip in my mind.

"I have to leave after dinner to do some work." He let those words hang in the air, and I didn't respond because I knew he wasn't finished. He slowly took a long drink of his vodka and then set the glass on the table, keeping his hand wrapped around it, his index finger slowly tapping against the side in an almost hypnotic way.

"Okay," I said a little too breathily and then felt my cheeks heat. I reached across the table for my glass of red wine, the exact opposite of what I should've been drinking. After I took a drink and set the glass back on the table, a heavy weight of silence moved between us.

"I don't have to ask that you stay in the apartment while I'm gone, right?" His voice was low and firm, as if he was trying to be as nonthreatening as possible. And although this man was dangerous on every level, I knew he wouldn't hurt me.

Stupid, stupid girl.

"I'll stay in the house, because I know it's dangerous, but we do need to discuss me going to work tomorrow."

He didn't move, said nothing, but I saw the subtle tightening of his jaw after I spoke.

"We'll talk about it," he said, and now it was my turn to clench my teeth together, because his tone felt strangely like he'd only said the words to placate me.

I wanted to instantly lash out. I didn't need another father. And although mine was worthless and the world wouldn't miss him if he was gone, I also didn't need anybody to look after me. I could do that myself. No one could take care of me better than *me*.

So although I wanted to stay on the subject, because that's what I did—fight—how I survived, I had to pick and choose my battles. I didn't have anywhere to be tonight, and I felt safe here. With Arlo. He was helping me by training with me, showing me how to protect myself. But I did repeat in my head a mantra I'd said over and over again, that I would get answers from him one way or another. Eventually.

It was another twenty minutes before I finally finished my dinner. I'd never eaten so well than when I was with Arlo, that was for sure. I'd never been full, always feeling that sliver of hunger biting at the edge.

And the entire time I'd been eating, Arlo had watched me. As if he couldn't take his eyes off me. I didn't know whether to be flattered or if he thought there was something wrong with me, but I chose the former, because the things I felt toward him with just a glance, things that made my belly tighten and my heart flutter, couldn't handle rejection, not with the way my life had been going.

I finished off my wine, the alcohol giving me a warm sensation, my limbs feeling a little heavier than normal.

"Come here, I want to show you something." He

stood and walked past me, and I had no choice but to follow.

We made our way through the living room to the other side, where the shadows seemed thicker, where the lighting didn't penetrate. He stopped at a sliding glass door I hadn't even noticed, it was so seamless with the rest of the windows.

When he pulled it open, the night air washed in, teasing the strands of my hair around my shoulders. It was chilly, but it felt good, my body temperature seeming stifling whenever I was near him. We stepped out onto the balcony, and I felt the breath leave me at the scenic view in front.

Although the city had been gorgeous on the other side of the windows, as I walked toward the balcony and curled my hands around the cold, hard edge, it now seemed so surreal.

The banister was made up of thick glass with steel framing, giving the illusion that you were closer to falling over the edge than you really were. It had my legs tingling and my knees buckling. It made me feel alive.

This high up, the wind was vicious, lashing out at you as if it were angry you'd dared to come out and experience it. I felt Arlo's presence as he came to stand next to me, but I couldn't drag my gaze away from the cityscape.

Even so high up, I could hear the faint trickling sounds of life down below. I could visualize people yelling at each other, honking their horns and waving their fists in their anger. I imagined lovers were whispering soft things in each other's ears and children crying for their mothers to buy them more sweets.

I could practically smell the hot dogs from the street vendors, the yeasty scent of the fresh bread that filtered out from the open doorways of cafés and bakeries. If I closed my eyes, I could imagine I was somebody else, somewhere else where nothing could touch me. And being stories upon stories above it all, it was an almost tangible feeling that it was true.

"I know you want answers," he finally said after a long moment of silence.

I turned my head to look at him, my upper body leaning against the banister, the wind now more of an intimate caress.

"But you being dragged deeper into this—into a darkness that is unforgiving—comes with a price." His eyes looked so dark under the moonlight and

backlit by the cityscape. "I don't think you understand how—"

"Dangerous it is?" All the *whys* bounced in my
head, but they didn't make it past my lips. I found
my gaze drifting lower. His mouth had tipped up at
the corners slightly as I'd cut him off, but he still
finished his sentence.

"Something like that." His voice wrapped around
me, pulling that invisible thread between us tighter
until I feared it would either snap before we made
contact or irrevocably keep me ensnared.

I forced myself to look back into his eyes, trying
to wade through the fog that had suddenly filled my
head. "I can handle precautions. I can even handle
violence." *I've seen enough of it.* "I just don't want lies."
I didn't know what I meant by saying those words,
but his expression told me maybe *he* understood.
But still he said nothing, and I felt like the flickering
in his eyes told me he couldn't promise me the truth
regardless.

I cleared my throat and faced the city again, a
shiver taking hold of me tightly. "Would it be
possible to go to my apartment and grab the rest of
my things?" I didn't know if I expected him to tell me
I'd go back there soon so there was no need to get
my stuff, but he kept quiet for so long I glanced back

at him. He was still watching me, but the look on his face was conflicted.

"Tell me what you want, and I'll stop by and grab what you need."

Now it was my turn to stay silent for long moments. "No offense, but I usually wait until the third date before having the guy riffle through my underwear drawer," I teased, but the way his pupils dilated after I spoke had any humor leaving me. His expression was so intense that I felt goose bumps move along my arms and legs. I shivered again.

When he reached up and smoothed his thumb along my cheek, I closed my eyes and leaned into his touch. He felt so good, his skin warm, his hand big.

"Ya by ubil lyubogo, kto pytalsya zabrat' tebya u menya."

I felt my heart race faster at his words. I didn't know what he said, but he whispered it so deeply, with so much possessiveness laced within, that I knew whatever he'd just spoken was the absolute truth.

"Did you just say I wasn't worth all this trouble?" My voice was light, or at least I was trying to make light of the sudden heaviness I felt.

He didn't smirk, didn't do anything but stare at my lips, ones I suddenly felt like licking. "Let me know what you need, and I'll make sure you get it. Whatever you need," he said deeply, his gaze still on my mouth.

And then he turned and left me standing there, and a part of me knew he'd forced himself to leave, because if he hadn't, I was pretty sure this night would have been ending a hell of a lot differently.

Like with me in his bed.

16

Arlo

I'd gotten the text from Dmitry this morning.

Butcher and Son. Midnight.

A part of me wasn't going to go. I didn't owe the bastard anything. I didn't work for him or his father, yet a dark curiosity filled me on why Leonid's oldest would want to speak with me. And if we were doing this at the old slaughterhouse, it was clear he didn't want a witness. He didn't want the Pakhan to know.

I pulled my car around the back of the old building and cut the engine. I grabbed two guns, a GLOCK and a Beretta, and tucked one in the waistband of my pants and the other in the front. I adjusted my jacket and climbed out, already having three knives strapped to my body, hidden yet easily accessible.

I didn't trust any of these fuckers.

As soon as I stepped in the warehouse, I felt eyes on me and found Dmitry leaning against one of the rusted walls to the sides. The shadows hugged him like an old friend, welcoming him back to the fray.

Tendrils of smoke curled around him, the end of his cigarette lighting up in the darkness, a flare of brilliant orange as he inhaled. He exhaled, those tendrils turning into a thick cloud in front of his face before dissipating.

Although I only saw Dmitry, I knew his brother was close. They were never far from each other. At only a year apart in age, they acted more like twins than siblings, knowing what the other thought, what the other felt, how they'd react. It was fucking eerie.

"Your brother can crawl out of whatever dark hole he's occupying anytime now." I kept my voice low, but I knew it was loud enough Nikolai would hear. I made my way toward Dmitry, watching for any subtle changes in his posture, listening to the sounds around me to gauge where his brother was.

The Petrov brothers were young, in their early twenties, yet I knew they'd experienced much of the same depravity of the underworld as I had. It had hardened them, made them lack any normal empathetic, human feelings toward others. It had pulled that light that could've grown in them completely away until there was no chance they'd ever grasp it.

That's how I'd been, how I'd felt. I had always assumed I'd die in a dark hole where I'd forever be alone, the dirt covering me up so I'd never have the chance to crawl myself out of it.

I thought of Lina back in my apartment. *Moy svet. My light.* She made that light attainable, reachable. *Real.* And that's why I'd do anything—everything—I could to ensure my world didn't touch her.

I could hear Nikolai's low laugh somewhere close by, echoing off the rusty, debilitated walls, but I kept my focus on Dmitry. When I was a few steps from him, I watched him inhale again, that smoke circling him, clouding his visage. Yet his eyes positively glowed as he stared at me.

He leaned against the wall with one leg crossed over the other, one hand tucked into his pants pocket. He flipped the ash from his cigarette, took one more hit, then flicked it away before pushing off the wall and coming to stand before me. His lips peeled off his teeth, all straight, white, and flashing in the darkness.

"My father has been talking nonstop about the

scene you caused the other day." He let those words hang in the air between us. And so did I. "I swear he's got a constant fucking hard-on because of it. It's been a long time since I've seen him so excited about something."

I had no doubt Leonid was obsessing about the fact that I'd expressed so much emotion, especially over a woman. That's why she was at my penthouse, because I knew the fucker wouldn't give up until he figured out a way to take her, to use her so I would do what he wanted. And that was joining his army in the Bratva and just becoming another soldier, another one of his pawns.

He was twisted enough to hurt her to force my hand. And I wanted her too much that I'd do anything to keep her safe.

I heard one set of footsteps behind me. I knew it was Nikolai. He was even less of a threat to me than his brother and his father, although only because I was more skilled, more deadly and dangerous. I saw him in my peripheral as he made his way around me and stood beside Dmitry.

"I don't know whether to be offended or to up my game over the fact that you didn't even flinch in my presence," Nikolai said, and I looked in his direction.

"Probably safe to assume both."

Nikolai sneered in my direction but kept his mouth shut.

Both the Petrov boys were large assholes, as tall and as muscular as me. With matching dark hair and eyes, they looked more likely to grace a fashion magazine or be on the big screen than slithering around in the dark, killing and maiming in the name of the Russian mafia.

If their father was the gun, they were the bullets.

"Your father needs to find a hobby if my life is so consuming to him." I addressed Dmitry in reference to what he'd said about Leonid. I looked back at Dmitry and saw something flicker in his eyes, a hard calculation. But it was gone as soon as I'd seen it, washed away with a sharklike grin.

Long moments of silence stretched out, and my patience wore thin, my annoyance growing. I wanted to go back to Lina. I wanted to feel the softness of her cheeks again. I wanted to feel her lean into my touch. And these little fuckers were taking my time away from her.

"You need to get the fuck on with it and quit wasting my time." My voice hardened, my jaw tightening. My fingers twitched to grab my gun and aim it at Dmitry's head, to pull the trigger and put a bullet through his skull just to send a message to Leonid. I always was a trigger-happy bastard.

"I'd like to offer you a job."

I didn't hesitate to respond right away. "I already have a job with the Ruin." I could see the snarl on Dmitry's lips, but I didn't care if the fucker didn't like my response. "And even if I didn't, I wouldn't take a job from someone who barely has hair on his balls." It was a low blow, but I was agitated over the Lina situation and these assholes keeping me from her.

Dmitry laughed, deep and low. "Man, Arlo, if you were anyone else, I would have already put a bullet between your eyes for your insults."

I curled my lip. "You could *try*." Dmitry may have only been a decade or so younger than I was, and far from a child, but I'd seen more in my years in this fucking underworld than he'd probably ever experienced in his life, even being the son of the Pakhan.

"I'm going to give you a pass on the disrespect." He held up one finger. "But just this once, Arlo."

I curled my fingers tightly into my palm and bared my teeth. "Is that so?" I took a step forward and saw Nikolai tense. But Dmitry held his hand up, stalling whatever his brother was about to do.

"I think we're getting off on the wrong foot here." Dmitry tipped his head to the side as if trying to examine me, trying to figure me out. *Good fucking luck.* "I think this is something you'll like, Arlo, something that will satiate that evil, tar-stained, fucked-up soul of yours."

Nikolai gave a little chuckle in response.

And then the air shifted, changed as it charged with something sickly and vicious. The atmosphere wasn't lighthearted anymore, wasn't the soft laughter of a demented man with fake smiles and a twisted mind. It was a sudden seriousness that was cloaking, a sturdy presence like a fourth body in the room.

"We want you to kill our father." Dmitry said it so matter-of-factly that I was actually taken aback, his words so final there was no doubt in my mind he meant every single one. "I know, before you say it or even think about it, that you're wondering if this is a setup." He held his hands out, palms up. "This is my brother and me offering you an olive branch. We're giving you a chance to take out the threat that is directed at your woman, no strings attached, no repercussions with the Bratva. No retaliation."

I eyed them both, gauging their body language, sifting through it all to see if they gave away any signs. Sweating, shifting of eyes, twitching of bodies. But they were both cool and collected, their breathing easy, their focus on me.

Well, fuck me. They were dead serious.

I knew they had no real love for the man who'd fathered them, had heard plenty of stories of their upbringing and all the vicious shit Leonid did to "toughen" up his sons. Where he treated his daughter like a princess, a little bird in a gilded cage, his sons got the blunt force of his brutality.

I chuckled, but it held no humor. "You little shits think you can take down Leonid on your own?" I lifted an eyebrow as I eyed them both. "I'll give you both credit; you have some balls of steel, conspiring to take down one of the strongest Pakhans in the Bratva."

"He's become unorganized, his vengeance with the Cosa Nostra becoming volatile. He's making too many mistakes and fucking things up. He's going to end up bringing a lot of fire and death down on this organization and ruin a lot of connections we have in place." Nikolai was the one to speak, and I was surprised by the thought-out response. He actually sounded clearheaded and not like a raving lunatic.

I'd always heard Nikolai was more of the party-goer in Petrov's trio, the one less likely to give a shit about following in his father's footsteps. The responsibilities fell more on Dmitry for obvious "oldest son" reasons.

"I'm not sure how this is my problem," I responded, feeling the need to go to Lina even stronger than before.

Dmitry gave me a hard smile. "This is *your* problem, because my father has plans for your woman."

My entire body tightened, even though I already knew Leonid wouldn't leave this alone. I'd seen the excited glint in his eye as I took Lina out of his bar.

"I don't need you or your brother interfering."

Nikolai snorted and leaned back on the wall, crossing his arms over his chest and glaring.

"He's like a dog with a fucking bone over having you join the ranks." He shook his head. "I don't get his obsession with you, but he holds you in high regard and will use whatever means necessary to bring you in."

"And he plans on trying to use her as collateral to force my hand." I didn't phrase it like a question, because I knew that was the outcome Leonid saw. I knew the way the fucker's mind worked. Dmitry was quiet for so long it started to feel like this itch under my skin.

"I don't think you understand the obsession my father has with that woman. Because he knows you want her, because you couldn't control yourself, he won't stop until he makes you see his way of thinking." I saw a muscle in Dmitry's jaw tick, as if just speaking about how fucked up his father was almost sent him into a rage. "He wants to make her *his*, Arlo. That's the fucking truth of the matter." Dmitry took another step forward, and my entire body tightened. With readiness. I was already walking on a razor's edge and trying to control myself after hearing the news—the fucking threat—of what Leonid wanted with Lina.

I moved my hand suddenly to my back to get better access to my gun.

"Do you understand what I mean, Arlo? Do you understand what my father does to women?"

I gritted my teeth. I knew.

"He's a savage toward the fairer sex. Fucking deplorable."

I was surprised to hear the venom in Nikolai's voice as he spoke about his father. Although they may not have cared for the man in a father/son sense, I always assumed they had some kind of respect for him. It was very clear they didn't.

"He'll destroy her, Arlo, and I don't mean end her life in the most humane, painless way possible. He'll beat her down mentally and emotionally until she's nothing more than dough that he can form into whatever vision he sees fit. And when he's the only thing that she can grasp on to, when he has you right where he wants you, he'll destroy you too."

I was seething with rage, and there was no way I could hide my body's reaction. I wasn't even trying as a deep growl of aggression and warning left me.

Dmitry smirked, but it didn't hold the amusement or satisfaction I assumed it would from seeing me lose control. The very thought of anyone so much as laying a hand on Lina made me want to desecrate the entire city of Desolation. To think that somebody would touch or hurt her, to snuff out that light, made me want to go on a killing rampage.

"Our father needs to be taken out, Arlo. And because you now have a direct link to him through your woman, because she's a threat and you know my father won't stop until he gets what he wants, which is now both of you, she won't be safe."

I curled my lip at him. "Don't fucking act like you're giving me some kind of fucking gift, like you're doing me a favor. You're doing this because you want power, Dmitry. You're doing this because your father is psychotic and destructive, becoming too volatile apparently. Don't fucking act like you're giving a handout simply because you have a good heart. It's just as fucking black and soulless as mine."

Dmitry laughed and looked over his shoulder,

which had Nikolai chuckling as well. "As much as we'd like to take out the old fucker ourselves, show him the kind of family love he's shown us as we grew up, you know how our world works." He looked back at me. "It would be bad form for us to have a personal hand in it. But you're the best of the best. A real coldhearted bastard, aren't you? You could take him out and make it look like he just disappeared. Poof," he said as he curled his hand into a fist in front of his face.

I turned from them and paced, knowing what I had to do but not wanting to fucking work with Dmitry or Nikolai. I didn't want to make back-alley deals with them. This wasn't even about the Bratva or their Pakhan. I couldn't give a shit about Leonid and his fucked-up morals. My only concern and priority was Lina.

I turned to face them and growled out, "She's mine."

Dmitry started laughing. "Yeah, I think you made that pretty fucking obvious when Dima touched your girl and you pulverized his fucking hands." Nikolai started laughing even harder this time after his brother spoke. "Although it served the fucker right. He was a touchy bastard and doesn't know what the word 'no' means."

I clenched my jaw so tightly I wouldn't have been surprised if I cracked some teeth. As I stared at the dirt and trash strewn on the ground, the stench of decay and age surrounding me, I knew what I had to do.

"You and I both know you're going to take him out." The confidence in Dmitry's voice made me instantly want to break his neck, but I said nothing, just glared at the prick. "My brother and I don't need more war. We want an alliance between the Cosa Nostra and Bratva. We need to grow stronger and create not only domestic deals but international ones. And we found a way to do that. But if our father stays in power, he'll destroy the progress we're making." Dmitry looked at Nikolai and smirked, as if they shared a silent conversation on what was really going down.

"Didn't you know?" Nikolai prompted and pushed off the wall, stalking toward me. "I'm getting hitched. Got an arranged marriage to a sexy little just-turned-eighteen Italian hottie." He wagged his eyebrows and grinned lasciviously.

"That's your plan? An arranged marriage between the Petrov Bratva and Cosa Nostra?" I ran a hand over my face and shook my head. "You guys are even crazier than I thought."

Dmitry grinned and didn't say anything else. Good. I wasn't into all the politics that came with the crime underworld. And I didn't want details and logistics on what was all going to go down.

"So we came to a father killer to handle this."

I kept my expression composed as I stared at Dmitry. They wanted their father out of the picture, wanted to fucking tie themselves with the Italian mafia, so that was *their* fight to deal with. But now Lina was in the mix because of me and my fuckup. I had to finish this. I had to go into the fold whether I wanted to or not, but when it came to her, I realized I'd do anything to protect her.

She had secrets, ones she'd tell me eventually, ones I'd take care of for her, so she never had to worry about anything again but being with me.

I'd do anything to make her mine. And tonight I was going to make her see—and feel—just that.

17

Galina

I woke to the groggy feeling that I hadn't been asleep for very long, the weight of that tiredness trying to pull me back under, but something had woken me up, so I forced myself to blink my eyes open.

I stared at the ceiling, a sliver of the ambient city light coming through the curtain of the bedroom window. As my mind cleared and I woke up further, I realized what had roused me.

I wasn't alone.

I felt someone watching me, and my gaze was pulled to my side of the bed, where I saw a large masculine body sitting, his forearms braced on his thighs, his head cocked to the side, and his eyes latched on me.

I gasped and sat up, knowing it was Arlo as the fog in my mind cleared. With a hand on my racing heart, I licked my lips and let the silence stretch out between us.

"Moye serdtse bolit, kogda ya smotryu na tebya." His voice was deep and low but still had the intense effect of moving over every inch of my body and lighting it up.

"Arlo?" I whispered his name in the darkness. "What's wrong?" It wasn't by the way he watched me, but the tension in his shoulders, the way he clenched his jaw so tightly I could all but hear his teeth grinding. "Is everything okay?" Every little shift I made on the bed was followed by his eyes, as if he was tracking me and refused to let his prey go.

"It will be," came his reply.

My heart thundered at those three words that sounded almost threatening. But not to me. *Never to me*, I thought with certainty.

I'd put my hair in a loosely knotted bun after my shower, and a strand tickled the side of my face. I pushed the lock away from my cheek, seeing Arlo watch the act with a clarity that was startling.

After he'd left for the night, I stayed on the patio

for so long my fingers had felt like ice before going numb. I'd taken a too long and too hot shower, then slipped into bed, where I was sure I wouldn't have been able to fall asleep because I felt too wound up, my thoughts too consumed with Arlo. He'd been on my mind a lot before all this drama happened, but now being in his home, surrounded by the constant sight of him, the masculine way he smelled, and coupled with our almost intimate self-defense classes, I couldn't *stop* thinking about him.

I glanced at the small clock on the bedside table and realized I'd only been sleeping for an hour, and although I'd been groggy upon first waking and still very much tired, my body had woken up like a firework exploding in the sky with each passing moment in his presence.

I was confused why Arlo was here... so close and watching me so intently.

"I'd like to take you out to dinner tomorrow night," he finally said after a long moment of passing silence.

My heart raced faster than it should at such an innocent statement, and I found myself licking my lips. He was so close that I could reach out and touch the stubble along his chiseled, square jaw. "Dinner? Like a date?" I felt stupid right after the words left my mouth, and the way his lips twitched told me he thought it was funny, or maybe cute in a childish way. "Of course I didn't mean a—"

"Yes, Lina. I'd like to take you to dinner for a date."

My entire body hummed with pleasure. Going on a dinner date with Arlo shouldn't have made my body tingle the way it did, but here I was, feeling a blush steal over my face. "Okay," I whispered and ducked my head, this sudden shyness claiming me. A second later I felt the bed shift as he moved closer to me; then his finger was under my chin, bringing my face up so I was looking at him once more.

I glanced into his eyes that looked far too dark in the shadowy room. And the longer we stared at each other, the more I felt my breathing grow shallow.

"Dlya tebya ya sdelayu eto bezopasnym."

I almost moaned at the way his deep voice moved over me as he said the Russian words.

And as if he just realized he'd spoken in a language I couldn't understand, he murmured, "I'll make it safe for you, Lina."

"Galina." My real name fell from my lips almost instantly, and I should have been afraid about giving that part of myself to him. It wasn't safe, not with the running and hiding, but as I looked into Arlo's eyes, this inherent part of me knew this man would live up to his promise to protect me. *Even from myself.* "Please, call me Galina. It's my full name." Not a lie, but also not totally the truth. Yes, it was my full name, but I'd made it sound like Lina was a nickname instead of what it really was. *An alias.*

Things started to feel weird then, more electrified, a charge in the air that had my breathing becoming even more frantic to the point I felt lightheaded. When Arlo's gaze dipped down to my mouth, he moved his thumb along my bottom lip, a slow and steady stroking that had pressure and heat settling between my legs.

"Galina," he murmured in the sexiest way imaginable. My eyelids started to droop, to close on their own, as my nipples beaded under my thin T-shirt, as my pussy became wet. I ached in the best possible way *down there.*

"Look at me, *moy svet.*"

I couldn't help but obey his command as I opened my eyes, my eyelids fluttering. I held my breath as our gazes locked. I knew what was coming. *A kiss.* I didn't want to stop it, even though I probably should have. It would only complicate things in the long run. But I'd been thinking about his lips on mine for the last couple of months, and even obsessively since staying at his home. I wondered if his kiss would be soft or firm, gentle or aggressive.

I didn't care how it was. I wanted whatever he'd give me, virginity be damned.

"You should stop me," he said, but he was leaning in slowly, maybe to give me a chance to change my mind. I wouldn't.

"But I won't."

The deep, primal sound that rose up from the center of his chest had more wetness spilling between my thighs and had my breasts feeling sensitive and heavy. I wanted his touch, his hands stroking over every single naked inch of me. I wanted his mouth on my body, drawing out all the dark pleasure I'd only fantasized about.

He slipped his hand along my jaw to curl his fingers around the back of my neck, pulling me forward until our lips were now touching. The kiss was soft, barely any pressure, but God, it felt so good. And when a little moan spilled from me, I felt the tension escalate in Arlo's body.

He groaned, and his fingers tightened on my nape a second before he deepened the kiss, tilting his head to one side as he used the hold he had on my neck to move mine in the other direction. I parted my lips on a gasp, and he used that opportunity to slip his tongue along the seam before delving into my mouth.

His kiss was passionate and deep, his flavor heady and spicy. I could taste a hint of vodka coming from him, and I found myself sucking on his tongue, drawing not only the essence of that liquor from him, but also everything that was Arlo. A rough sound vibrated out of him, and then he was hauling me toward him until I straddled his waist, my thighs split as I braced my knees on either side of his muscular thighs.

I wrapped my arms around his shoulders, bringing my breasts flush with his hard chest. Could he feel my nipples? The twin, hard points hurt so bad, but in the best of ways. The sounds we made as we kissed were wet and dirty, needy and desperate. I certainly felt like I was drowning.

But what a way to die.

His hands were on my waist, his fingers digging into my flesh in a bruising manner that turned me on even more. I sat down fully on him, and a gasp left me as I felt how hard he was right against the most intimate part of me. His harsh groan sounded more animalistic than human, and the kiss deepened farther.

He slid a hand up my spine, tangled his fingers in

my hair, and a moment later he yanked on the strands, pulling my head back and breaking the kiss. I moaned at the pleasure and pain that dominant act caused.

Arlo had his mouth on my throat instantly, his lips at my pulse point, sucking and licking, his teeth scraping over my sensitive flesh as he gently bit down. I shuddered on top of him, felt the rhythmic pull of his lips on my neck, and knew there would be marks there come morning.

His mouth was everywhere, along my jawline, skirting over my lips, his tongue licking slowly at my cheek before sliding down the side of my neck. It was such a primal act, as if he was this feral creature trying to stake his claim on my body.

"Tell me what you want," he grumbled low, his voice sounding thicker, as if it hadn't been used in far too long.

I didn't think I could find my voice right now, so another moan rose up. His fingers tightened in the bun of tangled strands on the back of my head, and he grunted when I started rocking back and forth atop his lap.

"Tell me what you want, *who* you want to give it to you."

I gasped at the forcefulness of his words, but it

was such a turn-on I felt even more wetness slide out of me, the cotton barrier I wore sticking to my cleft.

His erection was hard and thick between us, moving over my panty-covered pussy. I only wore a thin shirt and no bra, my underwear and his slacks the only thing stopping him from pushing into me and giving me what I really wanted—Arlo deep inside me.

"I want *you*." The words came out before I could censor them, but now that he'd heard them, I was glad I hadn't tried to keep them in. "I just want you, Arlo."

His fingers tightened in my hair again as he groaned, and then he let go of the strands, and I pressed my mouth back to his. The kiss turned deep and passionate, as if we were trying to breathe each other in. And the entire time I ground myself on him, rocking back and forth, writhing on top of Arlo as he slid his hands behind me to cover the small of my back. He pushed up my shirt and cupped my ass cheeks in his big palms, giving them a light squeeze that soon turned more forceful.

"So fucking perfect." He squeezed even harder this time until I felt my eyes close on their own as dark pleasure spiked within me. "You're so fucking hot." He kissed me with more force, grunting against my mouth until I swallowed the sounds, giving him a moan in return.

Arlo curled his fingers harder into my ass, and I started really rocking back and forth, sliding my slit along his massive erection. I felt like he had a steel rod tucked behind his slacks. I could imagine how good it would feel... how much it would hurt for him to push all those stiff inches into me.

He pulled at my bottom lip with his teeth, licking away the sting he caused, and that's when I exploded. I let my head fall back on my neck, his fingers now pulling out the hair tie, letting my locks tickle the base of my spine, my skin feeling overly sensitive.

"Fuck yeah." He had my now loose hair wrapped around his fist, tugging it hard enough I cried out as the pleasure went impossibly harder. The sting of him pulling my hair coupled with the orgasm rushing through me had me crying out loudly. Embarrassingly. "*Christ*, give me more of those sounds."

I never wanted the pleasure to end. And when it started to fade and I sagged against his chest, I expected Arlo to tense, maybe close off from me again. What I didn't expect was for him to wrap his arms around me and just... hold me. It made me feel like he didn't want this moment to end either.

"So beautiful," he murmured as he slipped his hand under my shirt and started rubbing my back gently, soothingly. I rested my head in the crook of his neck, Arlo's scent so dark and spicy. I inhaled deeply, wanting to take another piece of him inside me. The deep sounds of his soft Russian endearments made me sink against him even more.

His words ran softly along my body before licking them away as soon as they landed on my skin. He gently moved his lips along the other side of my neck, sucking at the flesh, pulling it between his teeth before letting it go. I felt those tendrils of pleasure rise again despite having just gotten off.

"Arlo." His name was a strangled mewl from my parted lips. I never knew I could sound so wanton and needy before.

"I know what you need, baby."

The world tilted as I was suddenly flipped around and now on my back, Arlo hovering over me. His hands were braced on either side of my body, the shadows concealing the majority of his face. I found that darkly attractive. All I saw was the thunderous, stormy look of pure lust reflected back at me.

He leaned down and started kissing me deeply.

"So sweet." Arlo was breathing so hard. *"S toboy ya teryayu kontrol."*

I ran my tongue along his bottom lip, pushing against the seam before delving inside and dueling with his tongue.

"You make me lose control, Galina."

I made a small cry of pleasure at hearing him saying my full name.

"You're dangerous to me. My only weakness." The last part was so low I almost didn't hear.

We kissed harder, my hands smoothing over his big biceps, my pussy wet, my clit throbbing in time with my pulse. The sounds we made were incomprehensible, rough, and guttural. Never once had I felt so out of control. Never once did I need something so instantaneous and consuming as I did right now with Arlo.

"Arlo, *please.*" I didn't care that I was begging, pleading for anything.... for all he could give me.

I felt his hands slide down my side, past the edge of my shirt, his fingertips skating over the bare flesh of my thighs. I felt goose bumps form along my skin as he gripped the T-shirt and pulled it up. I rose enough to help him take the shirt off, the cool air puckering my nipples instantly.

He groaned deeply, flattening his tongue along

one peak and dragging it up and around. Over and over again. I let my body fall back on the mattress, my hair no doubt a tangled knot on the light sheets.

I gripped the comforter on either side of me, pulling at it as he worked on one nipple and then went to the other, back and forth, over and over again. He tugged and tweaked at the flesh with his teeth, the sting of pain heightening my desire even more.

"I can't think when I'm around you."

I felt the vibrations of his words grow inside me. I thrust my breasts out farther, whimpering when I felt him slide down my body. I missed his mouth on my nipples, but he cupped the mounds as if he knew where my thoughts had gone, massaging them, tweaking the tips with his fingers and thumbs.

"Open for me." It was a thinly veiled demand I complied with promptly.

I parted my thighs, the cool air washing over me, my pussy so hot, so wet that my panties were stuck to my folds. I should've been embarrassed Arlo was the first man to see *that* part of me, that he'd see how worked up I was.

I closed my eyes as I kept pulling on my bottom lip, the pain from that small cut and my constant tugging on the flesh heightening my pleasure further. He ran his hands up my calves, over my knees, and moved his fingers up my inner thighs until he framed my pussy. "Look at me."

I blinked my eyes open and stared at the ceiling for a second before I pushed my upper body up on my elbows and looked down at Arlo. My breath caught at the sight of him between my legs, the darkness in his eyes, and carnal need reflected back at me, making my heart skip a beat.

He smoothed a finger along the edge of the material, so soft, so gently that it was maddeningly erotic. And when he pulled the material aside, exposing me, I bit my lip hard enough I tasted the copper flavor of my blood coating my tongue.

"Oh fuck, Galina." I could feel the soft puffs of his breath moving over my now bared flesh. He slowly lifted his gaze back to my face. "Are you going to let me touch you *here*, lick this sweet spot?" He slid a digit up and down the edge of my underwear. It was an almost innocent graze, but it seemed so dirty, so erotic.

"Yes," I breathed out instantly.

He groaned and leaned in, the sound of him pressing his nose to the material making my lips part even more. And when he inhaled deeply, a gruff sound leaving him, a stab of desire tore through me so hard I actually lifted my hips and pressed myself against him.

"You smell so good. The most addicting thing I've ever been around." His fingers were tight on the skin of my inner thighs. "I wonder if this pussy is as fucking sweet as you smell."

I was all but hyperventilating at his dirty words. And while he kept his gaze latched onto my face, he leaned in that last inch, my panties still shoved aside, and flattened his tongue on my cleft, licking me in a drugging way.

I made a sharp sound in my throat at the feel of all that hot, wet heat, at the way he kept licking me from entrance to clit. Over and over again until I felt something tingle at the surface of my body and consciousness, readying to explode outward.

My belly was hollowing from the force of my breathing, and my arms shook from holding myself up. But I couldn't stop. I had to watch.

"Mmm," he hummed and sucked my clit into his mouth, causing my back to really arch, nearly forcing my eyes to close as the pleasure slammed into me. "I was right. Your pussy is so much sweeter than I could have ever imagined." He moved back down and circled my hole, pressing the thick muscle in slightly before retreating and going back to my clit. "Addicting. I'll never get enough." He sucked at my opening, and I moaned. "I'll need to have my face buried between these pretty pale thighs every fucking night just to get my fix."

Oh God. I was going to explode just from his words.

"Who's licking this little pussy?"

My mind was in a haze as I let his words filter in.

"Who's the only one who will *ever* kiss you here?" He emphasized that single word by doing just that, a soft, almost sweet kiss against my clit. "Who's the only man who will ever know how sweet your cunt is?"

My hands ached at how tightly I tugged at the bedspread. I couldn't form words as I watched him tongue me, over and over again until I was lost in the sight of him doing these carnal things to my body. This was the best kind of torment.

"Tell me, *moy svet*." Those four words were a demand right before he sucked my clit into his mouth and gave a hard pull that sent me over the edge.

"You, Arlo. Only you," I cried out as I came.

"Fuck yes." His words were muffled against my flesh as he sucked and licked, nipped and stroked. I moaned when I felt him tease a finger along my pussy hole, my body tightening when he gently slid it inside me. "So fucking tight." He sounded like he gritted those words out through clenched teeth.

He sucked my clit again as he did a slow thrust of his finger in and out of me. And when he added a second, the stretch and burn, the discomfort of having something inside me for the first time heightened my lust.

I bowed my back, my breasts thrusting out, my nipples tight and aching. I buried my hands in his short dark hair and tugged at the strands as hard as he'd pulled at mine. It was on the tip of my tongue to tell him this was my first time... for anything, but I was so lost in the moment that all conscious thought was gone. Pulled out of my head as if it never had a place in there.

I came again, my arms giving out as I fell back on the bed, my hands slipping from his hair, my breath stuttering out of me. I let the pleasure wash through me until I was too exhausted to move, let alone ask Arlo to hold me.

"Look at me," he said low, deeply.

I forced my eyes open and lifted my head to watch as he pulled his fingers out of me, my arousal glistening off his digits. He spread them along my inner thighs, the warmth of my pussy juices cooling almost instantly along my flesh. He leaned in and dragged his tongue along all that cream, lapping it up like he was starved for it.

He pulled back, made sure my panties were in place, adjusted my shirt down so I was covered, and then he was pulling me into his arms. My chest was right on his, and the sound of his frantically beating heart had me smiling. He might act outwardly like he was fine, controlled, but he couldn't hide this.

I shifted closer, and I felt how hard he was. I pulled back and tipped my head in his direction. "What about you?" He cupped the side of my face, his thumb stroking over my cheek. Arlo didn't say anything for long seconds, and when he leaned down and kissed me slowly and gently, I melted into him, tasting myself on his lips and tongue.

"This isn't about me. I didn't do this for you to reciprocate." He kissed my forehead and whispered, "Besides, eating that sweet pussy brings me more pleasure than you'll ever know."

I shivered, and he tightened his grip and pulled me closer to him.

"You're mine, Galina." His words sounded final. "*Ya ub'yu lyubogo, kto popytayetsya zabrat' tebya u menya.*"

"You've said that before. What does it mean?"

He was silent for long moments, and I could imagine he was trying to think of a lie, but what he uttered told me it was the absolute truth.

"It means... I'll kill anyone who tries to take you from me."

Galina

The next morning I found myself alone in bed, the covers over me, the other side of the bed cold, telling me Arlo probably left as soon as I'd fallen asleep. I didn't want to let that bother me as much as it did, but what we'd shared last night, what he'd done to me and what he'd said, made me feel even more connected to Arlo than ever before.

I got ready for the day. Our morning routine was the same with a danish and cup of coffee, but I noticed Arlo's gaze on me was even more intense than before. I couldn't stop thinking about his hands and lips on me... what he'd done between my legs, his mouth sucking and licking at me like he was so hungry for me he'd never get enough. I wondered if he'd thought the same thing.

And as I stood a few feet from him in the boxing ring, my heart thundering and sweat lining my temple, my physical reaction had nothing to do with what we were about to do and everything to do with where my mind had gone.

I was so aroused, and he hadn't even touched me today.

"You're not focused this morning," he rumbled low, his expression that same stoic mask that made it impossible to see what he could be thinking about.

"I'm fine." *Lie. Such a lie.*

He smirked and took a step closer, and my heart jackknifed in my throat. "That so?" I nodded but didn't trust my voice. His smile faded. "I don't like lies, Galina. And grown men know to only give me the truth."

I took a step back as he advanced. "Yeah?" That lone word was a squeak out of me. "And if they do lie?" Why was I playing with fire? I was going to get so damn burned. The ropes stopped my retreat, and I reached behind me to grip them, curling my fingers over their thickness, praying it kept me from crumpling to the ground.

He stopped a foot from me, his eyes raking up

and down my body. My breath caught because I for sure could read his expression now. Arlo stepped even closer until I felt his body heat seep into me. I thrust my breasts out, and his gaze dropped to look at my chest. He lifted a hand and ran it over his mouth, the sound of his palm scraping over his stubble turning me on.

"You want the truth?" There was a challenge in his words, and I nodded. "If you want the truth from me, I expect the same from you." He moved closer like a predator, and the ropes dug into my back even harder. That pain heightened my pleasure and reminded me of last night and how good the orgasm had felt when that agony and ecstasy slammed into me.

He reached out and curled his big fingers around the ropes right next to mine, our skin brushing dangerously close. I clenched my thighs together as a pulsing ache settled deep within. "What I say might scare you." His focus was on my mouth, and I wanted to kiss him so desperately.

"I've been scared enough times in my life, and none of them were when I was with you."

I swore I saw a flicker of surprise on his face before it was gone. He leaned in and rested his forehead against mine, and for just a second we both breathed the same air.

"I kill, Galina." His words were low. "I kill men who lie to me." He took a step back, maybe assuming after he spoke the words, I'd shut him out. I'd erect a wall between us from fear and hatred.

"Are they bad men?" I whispered.

"Yes. They are the same as me."

I swallowed, again having a feeling Arlo said these things to make himself out to be a villain, and although I'd never see him as a hero, the knight who rides in on a white steed and saves the day, I also knew the man standing in front of me saved me simply because he didn't want me to be hurt. And he was still protecting me.

I took a step toward him and placed my hands on his chest. I stared at where I touched him, wanting to be honest for the first time in my life, wanting to confide in someone I trusted. And although I hadn't known Arlo for long at all, a fleeting passage of time if I was being realistic, I could honestly say I'd never felt so safe with anyone else.

"I used to live in Vegas," I finally said, not meeting his gaze, just staring at my hands, because I knew if I looked at his face, I'd lose the courage to tell him any of this. "I never had a stable household. My father had a drug and gambling problem, one so bad he got in trouble with some pretty dangerous men." I internally snorted at that thought. Henry seemed so harmless compared to Arlo. "A couple of months ago," I said, softer this time, and I felt Arlo tense beneath my hands, "I was dragged out of bed in the middle of the night and taken to this man who my father owed." I licked my lips, hating that any kind of weakness or fear came through my voice, but it pulled me back to that night.

Arlo lifted his hands and placed them over mine, not pulling them away from his chest, just holding me. He was giving me silent support to continue, I realized.

"My father, the piece of shit that he was, offered me to this man in exchange to clear his debt." The dark sound that came from Arlo had me squeezing my eyes shut tight. I didn't want his pity or anger. I just wanted to start over. I wanted to escape that. "My father offered up my virginity to wipe his slate clean."

The air shifted around us, tensed as Arlo let those words really sink in. I did look up at him then, and the stormy, violent expression on his face almost had me taking a step back. But I knew he'd never hurt me. I knew that by the way he still kept my hands pressed to his chest, his thumbs stroking over them in a gentle, reassuring manner. I wasn't about to go into all the disgusting things Leo would have done to me before selling me off to other sick fucks.

"But I was able to escape when we got back to my apartment. And so I ran... I ran to Desolation and became someone new." I exhaled. "I don't know if I'll ever be safe, not when I can't see my father or his debtor letting me go." I looked into Arlo's eyes. "And that's one of the reasons I'm telling you, because I want you to understand that my life comes with a lot of baggage, and the last thing I want is for you to deal with even more shit than what's already happening."

Arlo cupped my cheek and just stared at me for long seconds. He leaned in and kissed my forehead. I closed my eyes and sank into his embrace. "I'm sorry."

I felt my brows pull low. "Why are you sorry? You didn't do anything wrong."

He kissed me again before pulling me into the hardness of his chest. I rested my cheek against his heart and listened to the steady beat as he ran his hand up and down my back. "I'm sorry you had to experience the darkness of what this world offers. I wish you never had to be part of that." There was so much sincerity in his words that I felt the prickling of unshed tears in my eyes. "No one will ever hurt you. I'd never allow it, *moy svet*."

I believed him. God help me but I believed him. That's why I'd said anything about my past at all.

"What does that mean? I've heard you call me that a few times. Please don't tell me it means I'm too much trouble." I tried a teasing approach after such a heavy topic because I didn't want to speak about the shitty past anymore. I wished I could rip all of it from my world and never have to worry about anything but enjoying this one life I had.

Arlo was silent for so long I wondered if he'd ever answer. But then he cupped my face and leaned in to kiss me almost sweetly against my lips. "It means 'my light.' That's what you are to me, Galina. You're my light in all the darkness that surrounds me."

19

Galina

After confiding in Arlo this morning, the rest of the day had been filled with this weird energy. We worked out with more self-defense training, but the energy had just been off. Arlo seemed tense, a little distant, and it was clear he had something big on his mind. I didn't want to think it was about what I'd told him. I didn't want to obsess and worry that I'd pushed him away with what was following me, no matter what he said or what endearments he called me.

He'd taken me back to his apartment after we finished training, where he told me to relax until dinner but that he had business to take care of and would be back later. He left with another kiss to my forehead before leaving me standing in the foyer, staring at a closed door and having the horrible feeling that I'd pushed away the first man I'd fallen for.

And I had... fallen for him.

I now stared out the window of his Mercedes, the night having fallen an hour ago, my worry still at the forefront of my mind. I glanced over at him, but he was once again hard to read. He'd closed off from me, put that wall up so it was too solid for me to get through. A part of me just wanted to cancel tonight, because whatever bond I felt we'd started to share, the intimacy that I craved, was slipping through my fingers.

The restaurant Arlo was taking me to was a short drive from his apartment and still within the heart of the wealthy district of the city. I was glad he hadn't taken me back into my side of Desolation. He pulled to the curb, where a young man dressed in valet attire helped me out of the passenger side, and another man in the same uniform took the driver seat before pulling from the curb to park the car. Arlo placed a firm, warm hand on the small of my back and led me inside. I felt that touch through my entire body and glanced down to make sure my arousal wasn't betraying me through my clothing in the form of hard nipples.

Fortunately I was safe for the time being.

Arlo had told me to wear something more formal for tonight, so I'd picked one of the dresses he'd gotten for me. It was a black, thick, ribbed-knit, long-sleeve dress that fell to my knees. The gray wool jacket that had been among the clothing he'd splurged on for me, and the dark tights covering my legs protected me from the chilly, nearly winter air of New York.

Vasyli's looked like one of the many skyscrapers in this part of the city, but the brickwork and artistic flair were very much Russian. The cathedral depiction etched into the massive red double doors was so detailed you could tell whoever created it had put their heart and soul into it.

Rectangular windows were in even intervals along the front face of the building, ornate golden wrought iron covering most of the glass so you couldn't see inside. But the metalwork was so delicate and beautiful that it was almost prettier to look at than the open sky itself.

Arlo opened the door for me, and I stepped inside, the warmth of the restaurant and the sights and smells bombarding me in the best ways. Traditional Russian music played softly overhead, and the scent of savory and sweet food filled my nose every time I inhaled.

An older gentleman came forward, his smile big and adding even more wrinkles to his face. He looked more like a grandfather than anything else, especially with his thick cable-knit cardigan over his white button-down shirt. He had a full head of white hair, his eyes so blue and light they almost seemed transparent.

The older man and Arlo started speaking Russian, but I never felt left out even though I couldn't understand them, not with Arlo's hand still resting on the small of my back, his body pressed close to mine. After a long moment the older man turned to me and introduced himself as Akim, welcoming me to his restaurant. He kept a respectful distance, and I wondered if it was the way his gaze lowered to where Arlo's hand rested possessively around my waist.

We were led through the restaurant, and I took in the vibrant red booths on either side of us. A row of four-seater square tables was lined in the center of the room and between the booths. There were only a few people dining, and I assumed the lateness and that it was well past a normal dinnertime was the reason. But I liked that it was more intimate. I didn't think I'd feel as comfortable if the restaurant had been packed.

I was transfixed by the decor, at the very traditional and culturally aesthetic Russian theme. A gold Russian imperial eagle was front and center on the wall, vibrant colors splashed along the wings and spread out through the wall. A red and gold chandelier hung from the ceiling and cast an ambient, soft glow through the interior.

We were led to a booth in the back, and once at the table, the older gentleman asked me in a heavily accented voice if I cared for him to take my coat. Once it was off and hanging on the wall beside us, I slid into the booth across from Arlo. I felt nervous over this dinner date, or maybe it wasn't the date at all but everything I'd admitted to him this morning and the fact that he'd been acting off all day.

I hadn't realized I'd been so tense, but the fact that this was a *date* made me feel anxious even when it shouldn't, especially given all the things Arlo and I had done just the night before and the personal things I'd shared with him. But for some reason tonight felt more intimate than when he'd had his face buried between my thighs.

It was that thought, and the memory that followed, that caused a rush of all the feelings he evoked inside of me, which in turn had my body heating. I glanced up at Arlo and saw the way his eyes became hooded, as if he knew exactly where my mind had gone. Then again, my body betrayed me and how he made me feel at every turn.

And then the time flowed so seamlessly, so easily, that I let myself fall into just enjoying myself. The hours passed as we ate all the Russian foods and talked about all the wonderful things.

We didn't order from menus in the traditional sense, but instead the chef created dishes for us, and everything I tried was delicious and totally new to me. I sampled *pelmeni*—flavorful Russian dumplings. Then there was *borscht*—beet soup. I had a special fondness for the *pirozhki*, which was baked bread stuffed with meat, mushrooms, rice, and onions. This was all eaten between sips of vodka and incredible conversation with the only person who had ever made me feel comfortable. I forgot all about the weirdness that had come from Arlo all day. I forgot about all my problems and the shit that followed closely at my heels... the things I was running from.

It all felt so... normal.

By the time we had desserts—yes, plural—I was satiated and full and didn't think I'd ever smiled as much. My cheeks hurt, and my face felt hot from the vodka and smiling. I glanced around and realized we'd been here for so long, lost in just enjoying each other's company, that the restaurant had pretty much emptied. Meaning it was literally Arlo and me.

I leaned back in the booth and just stared at him, feeling my heart flutter strangely in my chest. I could have blamed the alcohol for the heat in me, or the way I couldn't stop blushing and grinning. But that wasn't the truth.

I was falling for my Russian, and I didn't want to stop, not even if the ground rushed up to greet me painfully. Not even if it killed me in the end.

"Tonight was wonderful. Thank you." His smile was slow and very satisfied. "I have never had such a great time." It was the sad truth, but one I owned.

"I'll have to make sure you experience so many wonderful times that it'll take away all the bad ones."

My throat tightened with emotions I didn't—shouldn't—think too hard on.

I didn't know what to say, but even if I found words to convey how he made me feel, the sound of the front door opening and the gust of chilled air rushing into the restaurant that made its way to our table would've cut me off.

I lazily glanced toward it, wondering who was coming to eat so late. It had to be going on midnight by now. My heart lodged in my throat, and I straightened, sensing Arlo taking full attention of my sudden shift in demeanor.

I glanced over at him to see this hardness come into his eyes as he glanced at who'd just entered. Leonid.

He had two barely legal women on either side of him, and when he noticed us, my breathing became shallow. It was the familiar dread I felt when I knew I was in the company of someone truly evil. His cold, dead eyes slid over to me, and he grinned slowly. I'd barely had any interaction with this man, only the small "interview" we'd done before I waitressed at his bar. But as I looked into the visage of evil itself, I knew without a doubt Arlo had been right.

This man was bad and dark to his very soul, and he'd do *anything* to get his way.

The next few minutes happened in slow motion. I could see the way Arlo's entire body grew taut when Leonid walked past our table, but his expression was surprisingly stoic, as if he was masking his true feelings even if his body reacted on its own. Leonid only gave Arlo a moment's glance before his focus was right back on me. I didn't miss how he curled his hands around the women's waists even harder, so hard I didn't miss the slight winces that covered their perfectly made-up faces.

The way he raked his gaze up and down my body made me feel dirty, like a barrel of oil had been spilled on me and I'd never get it off. My skin felt itchy, prickly, the urge to scratch, to tear it off almost too strong to ignore. And just before he walked out of our sight, he winked at me as if it was a promise of what was to come.

"I think I want to go now," I said softly as soon as we were alone again.

Arlo said nothing as he paid our bill and helped me into my coat before leading me outside. His big palm was warm and steady against the small of my back. Once I was seated in the passenger seat, he crouched on his haunches, surprising me. His hand on my thigh was hot and heavy, and it gave me the sense of being safe. Because I knew these hands had killed so many.

"Do you kill people for a living?" I whispered the

words, not sure why I was asking him that right here and now. But they spilled from me like a wound opening up and bleeding out.

Arlo didn't speak for so long I was afraid I'd ruined the night, that he'd never answer. Things had been so off today after confiding in him; then they felt right again during dinner, as if whatever he'd been thinking had drifted away and he was able to relax.

"I think you already know the answer to that," came his reply.

I nodded slowly. Yes, I did know the answer, and it didn't send fear through me, didn't have me looking at him in a different light. "And you'll kill someone who means to hurt me." I didn't phrase it as a question because I knew he'd killed the drunk for me, to keep me safe, to make sure it never happened again. So I knew the answer already, yet I wanted him to verify, to tell me again... to show me I was as twisted as he was, because I *wanted* that confirmation.

He stroked my cheek so softly, so gently that it went against the very makeup of who he was, of who I saw him to be on the outside. A part of me knew this man was good—not inherently, not down to his soul, yet he was gentle to me, kind even. He treated me better than anyone else ever had.

"I'll never let anyone hurt you again." Back and forth, his thumb on my cheek was lulling.

Long moments we just stayed there, this strange, comfortable sensation filling me. It was as if this was where I had always been meant to be.

"I forgot something inside. I'll be right back." His voice sounded off, too low and calm... too restrained. He handed me the keys to the car. "Start it and stay warm. Keep the doors locked, although no one will bother you." He said it with such certainty and conviction I couldn't help but believe him.

He looked at me for a long second and then reached out to cup my face. I instinctively leaned into his touch and let my eyes close.

"Everything will be okay." I opened my eyes, not sure what he was talking about, because so much was *not* okay. "I'll make sure of it." His stare was hard. "You believe me?"

I was nodding before I even realized I'd done the act. My body already knew without a doubt this man's word was true. He leaned in and kissed me passionately, fully. He ruined me in the best of ways. And when he broke the kiss and stood, shutting the door and looking through the tinted glass as if he saw right into my soul, I knew it all so clearly my breath shuddered out of me.

I'd always be safe with him, and that should have terrified me, because it just meant Arlo was even more dangerous than the monsters that were after me.

20

Arlo

Not taking out Leonid just moments before, as he'd been far too close to Galina—as he'd looked at her as if he was undressing her with his eyes—had taken every single ounce of my fucking willpower.

I didn't want to leave her in the car, even though I knew she was safe. No one would fuck with her in this part of town. No one would dare even look in her direction, knowing she was with me. This part of Desolation was heavy Bratva territory. Which meant crime that didn't have to do with the Russians was damn near zero.

I stepped back into Vasyli's, seeing Akim speaking in a low voice with the bartender.

Akim glanced over his shoulder to see who'd entered, and at the look on my face, the silent command I gave him, he nodded slowly and walked over to the front doors, sliding the lock in place and tipping his chin toward the back, indicating to the bartender it was time to leave. Although he didn't know *why* I was here, I made my expression pretty fucking clear.

Shit was going down, and if he didn't want to be in the crosshairs, it was time to make himself scarce.

After meeting Dmitry and Nikolai at Butcher and Son and fully hearing their plan where their father was concerned, I hadn't needed to think about what had to be done. There was no choice in the matter. I'd planned on taking Leonid out even before speaking with his sons. The *how* just hadn't been planned yet.

Leonid had to be taken out in order to keep Galina safe. I didn't give a shit about the Petrov family's internal power struggle or what they had going on behind the scenes with the Italians. My only concern was making sure the woman who was mine, who I'd protect with my life, was never put in harm's way. Especially because of me.

Dmitry had told me his father came to Vasyli's every week at the same time and always took the private back room for his meal. After his meal—and a couple of forced sexual acts from the women he brought with him—he'd go back to his apartment, which was heavily guarded and had too many witnesses, and do unspeakable things to the females until they limped home the next morning, bruised and sore and destitute in ways they'd never imagined.

But here, at Vasyli's, he was unguarded, too arrogant in feeling he was safe in this part of the city. And that was true for the most part. But not tonight.

I hadn't wanted Galina to go anywhere near Leonid, because it would rack up my rage even higher. I hated having her near him, but this was the quickest, most convenient route to get this shit done with Leonid. I didn't want to wait, and neither did Dmitry or Nikolai. Waiting would just make the risk of Leonid finding out even greater... if he didn't already know. Not much got past the sadistic bastard.

At the thought of taking down Leonid, I felt a satisfaction fill me. I'd make sure it was the most bloody, brutal killing possible. He didn't deserve any less.

My anger rose so fast and high I was choking on it. The memory of Leonid looking at her, the fire in his eyes as he no doubt thought of all the ways he'd break Galina, had me curling my hands tightly into fists. I remembered the way she'd trusted me with the truth of her past—one I'd handle for her whether she wanted me to or not, one I'd take out once this was all said and done.

I'd hunt down the motherfuckers who thought to degrade and hurt her. I'd make them cry and beg for death before I gave them the final blow. I'd make sure Galina never had to live in fear again.

The bartender made himself fucking scarce like a fire had been lit under his ass. Akim disappeared as well. The heavy weight of silence was now the only thing that I let filter through my conscience. I had several guns strapped to my body, all concealed yet easily accessible. But that's not what I'd be using tonight.

Tonight, and just for Leonid, reserved for fuckers who personally wronged me, or in this case, the only important thing in my life that they wronged and threatened—Galina—I'd use my fucking hands. I'd make this intimate.

I wanted to see—*feel*—the blood flow out of Leonid's body as he looked into my eyes. I wanted my face to be the last thing he saw before he took his final breath. Just thinking about it got me off.

I could hear a few raised whispers coming from the kitchen, the clang and bang of pots and pans before total silence once again surrounded me. I made my way toward the back where the private room was, my heart a steady, calm beat in my chest, the thirst for blood surrounding me like a lover's caress.

The door Leonid was behind was shut, and I stopped in front of it, hearing the sound of a soft female cry on the other side, followed by the unmistakable clank of silverware hitting a plate. I knew the sick shit Leonid liked, how he got off on a woman's tears.

I unsheathed one of my knives and curled my fingers tightly around the hilt, the weight substantial, the blade sharp enough it would go through flesh seamlessly. With my other hand, I reached for the door handle and silently opened it, the hinges greased, everything still so silent aside from the unobstructed noises now coming from the room.

The interior had the same setup as the main restaurant with the Russian aesthetics, but there was only one white-linen-covered table set in the center topped with plates filled with different items. No one had heard the door open, not with the sound of one woman weeping and the other making the unmistakable sounds of giving head.

Leonid sat facing the door—never presenting his back and being vulnerable. His head was tipped toward the ceiling, his eyes closed, and one hand tangled in the hair of the woman giving him the blowjob. His hold was so tight in the strands that his knuckles were white, and there was no doubt the female had to feel that pain all the way down her spine.

I turned my attention to the other woman, who sat at the other end of the table, her wide eyes trained on me, her face tear-streaked, a bruise already marring her cheek. Blood had trickled out of her nose, and she hadn't bothered wiping it away, a crimson trail, a visual of the kind of pleasure Leonid got off on.

"Sosi eto, gryaznaya shlyukha." Suck it, dirty whore. To emphasize what he wanted, he lifted his hips with enough force the girl gagged, clawing at his thighs. She pulled back enough to suck in a lungful of air before she was right back to sucking his dick.

Leonid opened his eyes and righted his head, and our gazes locked. He wasn't surprised to see me here; that much was clear by the lack of emotion on his face, but then again, that's what I wanted. I wouldn't kill him unknowingly. I wanted him to know his life was ending tonight. It would give me even more pleasure.

He grinned slowly and pushed the woman away, her small body becoming unsteady before she righted herself and hurried to the other side of the room. He tucked his cock back into his pants and zipped it up, all the while staring at me.

In Russian, he said, "She's a poor substitute to the mouth I really want sucking my dick." He reached out and picked up an olive, popping it into his mouth before chewing it and washing it down with a swig of vodka straight from the bottle. He made a show of looking behind me. "I don't see that sweet piece of virgin ass to give me that visual, but" —he lifted his hand and tapped his finger on his temple—"I have her image seared right here. Makes fucking these sluts more fun."

I kept myself calm, didn't show any reaction. I didn't need to let my rage—which was paramount and tangible right now—control me. That's what he wanted. Leonid wanted me to let unused emotions make me sloppy.

"*Ubiraysya.*" The girls scurried fast as fuck out of the room, and once we were alone, I reached behind me and closed the door with a soft *click*, never taking my focus off him.

"Care to join me for a drink?" He picked up the vodka bottle and tipped it in my direction. "Seeing as one of us is going to die tonight..."

"I didn't come here for a drink."

He took a long swig and watched me before swallowing and setting the bottle back down. "No, you didn't." A long, terse moment of silence passed, one where I felt things start to escalate. "My sons think I don't know betrayal when I can smell it like a hound chasing a rabbit."

I kept my face emotionless.

"The little bastards were always a disappointment. I blame their weak whore of a mother." His smile was like the flash of a shark's teeth. "You came here because of the girl." He didn't phrase it like a question. He leaned back in his chair, the wood creaking from the shift of his weight. "Yeah, you came here because of the girl." He chuckled low and deep, and I knew I'd let my mask slip by the way he laughed harder and tipped the vodka bottle in my direction. "Not the sharing type, huh?" He shrugged. "I was never one to get attached. I like to keep my options open, and with so much willing pussy available, it's a buyer's market."

"Trafficking, forcing women to fuck you, or the fact that they are too afraid of your wrath to say no isn't willing pussy." I took a step closer, thoughts of Leonid forcing Galina to do anything rushing through my head in disgusting, vile clarity.

Leonid didn't speak, just kept that stupid fucking grin on his face. He held his arms out, his three-piece suit stretching wide over his chest. "Do you think you can take me down?" He slowly pushed himself up to his full height. His gaze flickered down to the knife in my grasp. "Hand to hand, eh?"

I kept completely still and at ease. I was ready for this. I pushed Galina out of my mind, the very thought of her having no place for what was about to happen. Without taking his gaze off me, Leonid started to unbutton his jacket before removing it and hanging it over the back of his chair. He moved around the table and took several steps toward me, stopping when he was an arm's length away.

For long moments we didn't speak, just held each other's gazes, the aggression and testosterone, the suffocating thickness filling the air. And then he struck like a cobra, his hand reaching for my neck. I had no doubt he planned to crush my windpipe, tear my trachea right from my throat.

I ducked and dodged right before he could wrap

his thick fingers around my neck. I thrust my arm his way, trying to lodge the blade into one of his kidneys, but he moved out of the way quickly, the knife grazing his shirt. I heard him hiss and knew I'd at least nicked the motherfucker.

We both stumbled back before I charged forward, my body crashing into his. I used momentum to push him backward and against the table. Plates and cups fell to the ground, glasses breaking, my boots crunching on the debris. We grappled for supremacy, with me trying to stab him, but the fucker was stronger than he looked, his arms corded with muscle, so he was able to block any hits.

"I'm going to have fun fucking the innocence out of Galina."

I felt this beast awaken further inside me when I heard Leonid say her full name. I shouldn't have been enraged that he'd dug up information on her, should have known the bastard would have wanted to cover all angles where she was concerned. His obsession wouldn't have let it be any other way.

I rammed my elbow into the side of his face hard enough his head cocked back and blood sprayed out. I used that moment to stab him in the side, his grunt of pain driving my bloodlust higher. Just as I was about to jerk the knife upward all the way to the motherfucker's heart, he slammed his fist into my gut with so much force the air left me and gave him the opportunity to push me back a step.

"You could have been my best soldier, could have been my right hand," he roared as he charged forward, but I tensed, waiting to absorb the hit, my fingers twitching on the handle that was covered with his blood. "What a fucking waste." His face twisted in rage, and I slowly grinned, letting him see the pleasure and darkness that consumed me.

This was why he wanted me as his weapon for the Bratva... because he knew I'd kill anything that stood in my way, and now, that was *him*.

Right before he rammed his shoulder into me, I turned and lifted my knee, connecting with his side and spinning around to wrap my arm around his throat. I shoved him forward so hard that when he crashed into the wall, a picture shook and then fell to the ground.

"You'll never hurt another woman again," I seethed, my mouth right by his ear. He jerked his head back, his skull connecting with my cheek. Fire raced along the side of my face, but I paid it no mind. The pain felt fucking good.

He bucked backward and was able to spin around, but I delivered a knee kick, causing him to howl in pain before he fell to the ground. I was on him in the next second, one hand wrapped around his throat, the other still holding my knife. I grinned wider as I delivered an elbow to his head. I watched the haze cover his eyes from the pain and disorientation, and I took that moment to lean in so our faces were close enough I could have given him a kiss of death before I ended this.

"Galina is *mine*, and I'll bring down anyone and anything who tries to take her from me." I bared my teeth in what I knew was a frightening display of the demon in me. "That even means you, you sick fucking bastard. I'm going to get off on slicing your throat open ear to ear." He struggled, but the hit to the head still settled, the glossy look in his eyes present. Blood trickled out of one of his ears, but the bastard had the balls to still grin, red covering his teeth.

"I would have fucked her until she was a broken—"

I brought my knife to the soft spot right below his ear and dragged it slow and deep all the way around until I reached his other ear, his skin opening up like a ribbon being pulled away from a gift. Blood sprayed across my chest and covered my hands, droplets splashing on my neck.

I straddled his waist and stared down at him, right into his eyes, watching as life faded from him as he struggled. His hands were at his throat like he could seal the wound up, as if it'd staunch the blood flow and save him. I kept my grin in place, because even though Leonid knew he was dying, even if he tried to use the last of his strength to push me off, everything he'd worked for was now nothing.

"Your legacy ends here and now, Leonid. Your sons will move in the opposite direction of what you wanted." I leaned in close so his blood was the only thing I smelled, that metallic scent that filled my nose and had adrenaline rushing through me. "Did you know they're forming an alliance with the Cosa Nostra?" Leonid's eyes widened, and he feebly struggled against the news. "Yeah, it seems like Nikolai is marrying a little Italian to bring the two families together." I laughed low at the look on Leonid's ashen face. "I bet that just skins you alive, doesn't it?"

His eyes narrowed in one last rush of aggression, and he grated out in a barely audible hiss, "Fuck. You."

I laughed darkly and cupped the side of his face before saying, "No. Looks like you're the one being fucked."

He started gasping, his mouth opening and closing, the blood flow from his neck slowing. And then he looked at something over my shoulder just as anything and everything that used to be Leonid Petrov faded away.

I stayed where I was as I stared down at him, this heaviness in my chest lifting marginally knowing Galina was safe from this fucker. I stood and walked a few steps back, and while keeping my eyes on the dead bastard, I grabbed my phone from my pocket and dialed the number that would handle the rest of this.

As soon as I heard the deep voice on the other end, I said, "I need to book a travel ticket for one. Yes, I need assistance with extra baggage." I stared at Leonid's now lifeless form as I put the cleanup in motion.

Once it was all set and my phone was back in my coat pocket, I reached over and grabbed a white linen napkin, rubbing it over my hands while I stared down at the fabric as it changed to red and pink. The blood of my enemy smeared across that strip of cloth, the stickiness of it covering my fingers and palms.

I let the napkin drop as I left the room, shutting the door behind me. If the women were smart, they were long gone by now. I walked down the hall and saw Akim standing in the kitchen entrance. His gaze took in the blood covering my clothing and hands. I gave him a nod, and he gave me one in return.

I left the restaurant and headed back to Galina. *Moy svet.*

My light.

21

Galina

I'd seen the blood on Arlo's hands and clothes, smelled it filling the car interior as he said nothing and drove us back to his apartment. I didn't need to ask what had happened... what he'd done. I knew.

He'd killed Leonid. He'd made it safe for me.

Arlo hadn't said one word the entire drive back, and not a single syllable once we were inside his penthouse. He headed straight to his room, and a moment later I heard the shower kick on. I'd wanted to go to him, to touch him, hold him—even if he probably didn't want that—and show Arlo I was here for him.

But instead I went to my room and showered. I had been able to still feel Leonid's oily gaze on my body, and wanted to scrub my skin clean until there was no memory of tonight left.

Now here I was, sitting on my bed with my hands clasped in my lap, my legs bare, and the only article of clothing I wore was a shirt that fell to midthigh.

I stared at the partially opened door, having heard the shower in Arlo's room turn off so long ago I'd been frozen in this spot, afraid to leave and talk to him, confront him... *comfort* him. But then I found myself pushing off the bed and standing, making my way out into the hall and to his room. The door was open, but he wasn't there, the bed made, the room void of life.

I heard a soft sound come from down the hall and walked on bare feet toward the kitchen. I stopped when I saw Arlo's huge form standing against the granite breakfast counter, wearing only a pair of dark sweatpants, his chest bare and so wide and big, so muscular and powerful.

He'd killed a man tonight with that body, with those hands.

I felt my heart flutter in my chest and was walking toward him before I realized I was doing it. He didn't look at me, although I knew he was fully aware I was moving forward. He brought a bottle of liquor to his mouth and took a long pull from it before setting it on the counter, the glass hitting the granite making a hard *clank*.

I was a few feet from him and held my breath as he turned his head, and our gazes crashed together, held so strongly I felt it in the pit of my stomach.

"Come closer," he said so low it felt like an intimate caress against my body. There was no doubt in his tone I was not to disobey. But I didn't move. I couldn't. Something held me back, maybe fear of these feelings inside me, maybe the unknown of what happened next. "Come here."

I was obeying him instantly after those two words spilled from his mouth, an anchor wrapping around me and tethering me to Arlo in a way that ensured I wouldn't drift again.

His hand shot out so fast that I had no time to react, to gasp... to run.

He curled his hand around my waist and jerked me toward him, then spun me around and pressed me against the counter, my chest flush with the unforgiving, cold granite. The feeling of his body moving close to mine, his heat searing me from the inside out, was euphoric.

The sound of his palms slapping the counter on

either side of me was loud, causing my ears to ring, my body to tremble. His warm breath tickled my ear, and I shivered and closed my eyes.

"You should have run," he growled. "You should have run so far and fast from me that you thought there would be no chance for me to find you." He used his foot to kick my legs apart, and I teetered against the counter to steady myself. I did make a sound then, one of shock and arousal at his forcefulness, at the fact that he was so clearly unhinged.

"You would have found me." The words were so thin, like a blade of grass in the wind, one you're barely able to grasp as it slips through your fingers.

He pressed his body flush with mine, and I snapped my eyes open at the feel of how hard he was, the thick rod nestled right between my ass cheeks, my shirt molded to my body and a barrier to what I really wanted.

"That's fucking right, Galina. I would have found you." He pressed against my ass slowly, steadily, showing me what he was working with. "There isn't any place on this fucking planet you could hide from me." He slammed so hard against my ass that I was pushed forward slightly on the granite, my palms sweaty, slipping against the smooth top.

I couldn't catch my breath. My pussy was soaked.

This forcefulness coming from Arlo, the dominance and the way he spoke like he owned me and no one would ever have me but him was a fire between my legs that spread outward and threatened to burn the entire apartment down.

"I wonder how wet you are right now. I wonder if I slipped my hands between your legs, if you'd soak my fingers."

I didn't speak, couldn't, so instead I lifted my ass and ground the cheeks against his erection. The material of his sweatpants and my cotton shirt, and the fact that I wore no panties, left little to my imagination on what he was sporting between his legs, not when I could feel every hard inch, every defined ridge.

He hissed against my ear, pushing the long fall of my hair over one shoulder and wrapping the strands around his fist, jerking my head farther to the side, keeping me stationed. He leaned down to lick my neck like some kind of creature tasting his meal. "You must like playing with wild animals, baby. You must like the risk of getting bitten."

I closed my eyes and moaned, a nonverbal affirmation that I wanted anything he had to give me.

"So tell me... tell me how fucking wet your cunt

is for my cock. Tell me how much your body weeps for me to fuck it."

"Why don't you find out?" God, I really did want to get bitten as I taunted Arlo, as I lifted my ass and moved it back down, over and over again, grinding myself against him as if I had any clue what the hell I was doing. I had no idea how to seduce a man, but the lack of control and restraint I could feel coming from Arlo told me my lack of experience didn't matter. He wanted me fiercely.

He was still and tense behind me, as if my words had shocked him, maybe even pissed him off because I was going against him. I had no doubt not many people did, not if they valued their life. But when a deep sound of pure lust came from him, I knew I'd won. I knew he wouldn't deny me, because whatever thoughts he'd been lost in before I'd come into the kitchen, before my presence dragged him out of the blood that covered his vision and mind, I was more powerful in this moment to have that wrought-iron will vanishing.

He pushed that turmoil down so the man who was behind me was one who would fuck me to let me know we were both here and alive and nothing could change that. Because even if we both had some part of evil in our lives that festered, right here and now, Arlo was mine just as much as I'd always be his.

And as he slid his hands over my arms and down my waist to grip my hips in a bruising hold, I knew without fault I'd never wanted to be broken more than I did right now.

For a long moment he did nothing but hold me, his hands like vises around me. I wondered if he was trying to talk himself out of it, tell himself this was a bad idea, that crossing this line would end up changing everything. I wanted to yell and scream, look him in the eye and tell him things were already changed. *I* was already changed. And it was because of *him*.

He growled. "I've always prided myself on being a man with control, that nothing could bring me to my knees—figuratively and literally. But where you're concerned..." He ran the tip of his nose over the side of my neck, and I tilted my head to give him better access. "Where you're concerned, I've never been more irrational or fucking crazed in my fucking life."

I felt him push my shirt up and didn't stop him. I *wouldn't* stop him for the life of me. The cool air moved over my bare ass, and when he leaned back and moaned at the fact that I wore no panties, I felt a gush of wetness slip between my thighs. Could he see how soaked my pussy was?

"*Jesus Christ*, Galina." More long seconds passed where he didn't move, but I could feel his gaze on me, could feel him tracing the lines and curves of my ass with his eyes as if he was memorizing them.

I glanced over my shoulder and saw his gaze slide to the small hummingbird tattoo I had on my hip, a tiny thing with its wings spread out and its back arched. Arlo reached out to smooth a thick, calloused finger along the ink.

"Hummingbirds can flash their colors but hide them as well," I said softly, this hitch in my throat. I didn't know why I felt the need to tell Arlo that, but the words spilled from me before I'd had time to stop them.

I connected with the small bird that had a pulse of twelve hundred beats a minute, a tiny thing that was still mighty, that could hide but be seen... fast and smart. I liked to compare myself to such a creature, one complex even if on the outside it appeared fragile.

My body shook as Arlo slid his finger along my skin before dropping his hand back to his side. His gaze, so dark and penetrating, had all thoughts leaving me aside from the wicked things I wanted him to do to me.

"More," he said in a voice so low it was almost menacingly.

I took in a shuddering breath and did what he said, spreading my legs an inch more, wanting him to look at my inner thighs, to see how they were glossy because I was drenched.

He let out a low hum of approval that sounded almost evil. It made me hotter. "Do you like taunting me, teasing me?"

I knew it wasn't a real question, not the way he phrased it. He curled a hand against one bare ass cheek, his blunt nails scraping over the flesh until I gasped from the sensation.

I reached out farther to the edge of the counter, curling my fingers around the hard stone, bracing, giving myself leverage and purchase. I rose up on my toes to offer myself more to him, my entire chest flush with the counter, my toes barely on the floor now. I gave him a silent invitation.

"Do you want me to lose control, *moy svet*? Do you want a gentleman or a monster fucking you for the first time?" His words were gasoline on the inferno inside me. I wanted it, however he gave it to me.

"I want the real you." I glanced over my shoulder so I could look into his eyes. I knew what I wanted. I knew how he wanted to give it to me. I didn't care about the pain. I *wanted* it. "I want the monster."

His eyes became hooded, his lips peeling back from his teeth in a feral display of alpha aggression and pure lust. Without taking his gaze off me, he smoothed a big palm over my ass, his hand so large I felt tiny beneath him, a little doll for this Russian beast.

"Spread wider. Let me see this little cunt so wet and ready to take my cock." He gripped the other side of my ass, spreading my cheeks at the same time I widened my stance. I could feel the cold air along my heated pussy and had no doubt he could see my slit.

"So fucking juicy, pink, and swollen." His words were low, and I could tell they were spoken to himself. "Tell me who this belongs to." He emphasized what he meant by slapping my ass, not hard enough to hurt but firm enough there was a dark promise of what was to come. "Fucking tell me."

"You," I said breathlessly, far too softly for him to hear clearly, I knew.

"Fucking say it louder." He gave my ass a harder swat this time, and I moaned through the sting.

"You, Arlo."

He hummed in approval and soothed the sting away by running his palm in slow circles over my ass. "That's right. I fucking own this ass." He moved his hand closer and closer to the part of my body that ached the most. My clit throbbed in time with my pulse, my inner muscles clenched for something substantial only Arlo could give me, and my legs were shaking from the adrenaline moving through my veins.

The need to feel his big, callused fingers sliding between my lips, teasing the bundle of nerves at the apex of my thighs, to cup my cunt in his masculine hand, was so strong, so fierce I nearly begged him with tears streaming down my cheeks.

"And this?" he taunted as he finally slipped his fingers down my cleft, purring like a content feline. "So *fucking* wet. You're drenching my hand, baby, your pussy juices sliding down my fingers all the way to my wrist. Isn't that fucking *filthy*?" I moaned and shivered. He leaned in so his mouth was by my ear again and said harshly, "What a dirty little girl you are, hiding this sweet pussy from me."

Oh God, I thought as I bit my lip, my teeth digging into my bottom one so hard that I felt the skin break and tasted the tangy, coppery flavor of blood along my tongue.

"Who does this sweet cunt belong to, Galina?" His fingers skated over my lips, massaging the tender flesh, sending shock waves through my core. He moved those big digits to my clit, rubbing slow, steady motions around it until I shuddered, so close to orgasming I could taste it. "Tell me who owns this, who you belong to, Galina, and I'll give you what you want." He added more pressure to my clit, and a low, threadbare sound left me. "I'll give you the world, every single fucking thing I am, baby."

"Arlo, oh God. You, Arlo. Everything I am belongs to you." I'd never been so free with my words and body, never meant anything as much as I did saying the words that spilled from my lips. But with Arlo, it was as if this dam had broken inside me, this rush of free falling emotions and feelings, sensations and desires. There was no stopping the torrent of carnal lust that exploded from me.

"So you're saying this virgin pussy is all mine? Mine to lick, to suck... to fuck as hard as I want?"

I tossed my head back and moaned loudly again, nodding before I moved my tongue along the wound on my bottom lip, continuously tasting that metallic flavor.

"Because this *is* my little virgin pussy, isn't it?

"Yes," I cried out as he rubbed my clit harder. "It's *your* virgin pussy." On any other occasion, I would've felt humiliated for saying such things, but I felt liberated as the words spilled from my mouth and as Arlo gave me an answering growl of approval.

"*Khristos.*" His voice was low, that one word harsh. "I'll never be the same because of you."

I didn't have time to think of what he meant by that, because a second later his body was off mine, and the feeling of his warm breath moving along my exposed pussy had my eyes snapping open.

I looked over my shoulder to see him kneeling behind me, his big hands covering each of my ass cheeks, spreading them wide, his gaze latched onto the private place he'd revealed.

"No other fucker will look at you *here* but me." It was a warning, as if he thought I'd tell him otherwise, as if I wanted anyone else.

I shook my head because I couldn't find my voice all of a sudden.

"Ask me for it." His voice was gruff, and I swore I felt the vibrations straight to my clit. I also didn't need to ask what he meant. I knew the dirty thoughts going through his mind. *They're the same ones running through mine.*

"I—" God, could I actually say the words? A resounding *smack* followed by searing pain in my ass cheek as he spanked me had me arching my back involuntarily. "Lick my pussy." The words whimpered out, pulled from me as if I knew what to give Arlo to have him give me more. But that didn't stop my face from heating hotter than the sun as the dirty words spilled from me.

His fingers were tight on my bottom, relaxing and flexing, as if he was just taking his time looking at what was nestled between them.

"I'm going to drown in you," he said a second before his mouth was between my legs and his tongue pushed through my swollen folds.

I gasped and moaned, my fingers painfully tight around the counter as I gave myself up to Arlo, as he drove me closer to the edge.

"Never enough." His words were muffled against my slick pussy. "So hot and sweet. You'll be so fucking tight gripping my cock as I fuck you, as I put my claim on this untouched cunt." He slapped my ass, and I curled my toes, my eyes rolling back, my body not my own right now.

He wasn't human. He couldn't be by the sounds he made as he ate me out, the gruff snarls, the way he pulled my pussy lips between his lips, sucking them, gently biting the flesh before letting it snap back into place as he went to the other side and repeated the action.

And when he flattened his tongue and moved from my clit all the way through my cleft, licking me slowly, savoring me all the way to my asshole, I felt the familiar tendril of my orgasm rush forward.

"I want to see you so unhinged that you fly so high I'm the only fucking thing that can keep you grounded." He moved a finger around my pussy hole before gently pushing it in. My body gave way, accepting the thick digit, weeping for more. I heard the sloppy sounds as my body latched on to that finger, feeling my inner muscles tighten around it.

He pumped inside me once, twice, then slipped another finger in on the third thrust, scissoring until the stretch and burn gave way to more pleasure. And while he started pumping in and out of my pussy, he rubbed my clit with his thumb, sending me high into the stars until I was consumed by light and heat and knew I'd never be sane again.

"I need..." I didn't know how to say what I wanted, yet it should have been so simple. I thrust back on him, sliding my pussy on his fingers, fucking myself in a wanton, uninhibited way. I'd always been so in control of myself and my surroundings, but just letting go was freeing, and doing it with Arlo was liberating. "I need to come, Arlo." My voice was a husky purr, thick and drugged sounding.

"Does my girl want to come?"

"Yes," I cry-moaned. "God, yes." At the moment I'd never needed anything more. I'd die without it, I told myself.

Lazy thrusting in and out of me. Slow circles against my clit. He was torturing me, prolonging this, when all I wanted was to explode and give Arlo —the only man ever—my pleasure.

"Then come for me," he growled at the same time he sank his teeth into the flesh of my ass cheek and started finger-fucking me faster, rubbing my clit harder.

The pain and pleasure cracked through me like lightning hitting a tree, an explosion of light and heat encompassing all of me. I came, my back bowing, my tits shaking as my entire body shuddered with an orgasm that had my knees buckling. My nipples hurt because they were so tight, the blood rushing below my skin, no doubt pinkening it up, making it ultrasensitive.

I came so long that I could only pant through it all. And when I sagged against the counter, when the sensitivity was too much, I mewled my protest. Arlo slid his fingers from me, and I heard him sucking. Looking over my shoulder with what I knew was a sleepy, satiated look, I watched as he licked my wetness from his hand while he stared into my eyes.

"I could live off your fucking orgasms."

My eyes flared as he kept licking my juices off. God, his hand was soaked from fingertips to wrist. That should have embarrassed me, but... it didn't. I rested my forehead on the counter, my eyes closed, breathing through the aftereffects of my climax. But in the next instant, Arlo had me pulled up, my back to his chest, one of his thickly corded arms tight around my waist.

"We've just started." He spun me around and all but ripped the shirt from my body until I stood before him totally naked, breasts heavy, nipples tight, and pussy still so wet. He didn't try to hide how he raked his gaze up and down my body, his focus lingering on the junction between my legs for so long I grew self-conscious.

"Even though it's dark in here," he said in a growly voice and looked up at me, "I can see that sweet little slit, can see your glossy arousal coating your thighs." He leaned in an inch and braced his hands on the counter on either side of me, caging me in once more. "And it's because of *me*." He hummed. "That does something wicked to a man, Galina, something primal and possessive." When he leaned in so our lips were a hairbreadth away, I wanted his kiss, needed it. "You know what I'd do to any man who touched you or so much as looked at you?"

I nodded slowly, feeling my pulse kick into overdrive.

"Say it. Say the words out loud so you can hear the truth."

My chest heaved up and down from the force of my breathing. "You'll kill them."

His smile was slow, self-satisfied. "I'd tear them limb from limb until there was nothing left." He stepped back so suddenly I exhaled fast enough that I grew dizzy.

And then I couldn't help but look down at the heavy length of his erection tenting his sweats.

"You want more?"

I snapped my gaze up and licked my lips. I didn't need to respond because he saw my answer in my eyes. He hooked his thumbs in the waist of his pants and pushed them down, his cock springing out from the confines of his pants, his dick bobbing twice before settling and pointing right at me. His length and girth had my eyes widening, because although

I'd felt how large he was, seeing it brought it into a whole new level of reality.

His cock had to be the length of my forearm and just as thick, too wide for my fingers to wrap fully around. I clenched my thighs as wetness spilled from me, and despite my earlier—very powerful—orgasm, I wanted so much more.

He reached out and touched my hip. At first it was gentle, but then he added pressure, his fingers digging into my flesh, pushing me down until I sank to my knees. With my head tipped back and my gaze on his face, I couldn't breathe because of his startling beauty, not the kind that was classic and soft, but more of Lucifer... a fallen angel.

"Look at it."

I lowered my gaze to his cock, so thick and long as he held it in his palm right in front of my face. The head was bigger than the shaft, wider and flared, the slit teasing me. My throat tightened, and my mouth watered at the sheer size of him.

He gripped the base of his cock hard and started to slowly bring his palm toward me, his fist tight around the girth. His hand was huge, and his cock matched that of the man who held it.

Once at the tip, he lazily stroked himself back down to the base. He did this twice more, my breathing becoming even harsher with every passing moment he erotically teased me. And then he slid his palm back up to the tip, pushing free a pearlescent drop of pre-cum from the slit.

"Go on," he coaxed. "Lick it off like a good girl."

I braced my hands on my thighs and leaned forward, my eyes locked on Arlo the entire time as I dragged my tongue over the slit. His salty, very male flavor exploded on my tongue, and I couldn't help but moan. And aside from the tightening of his jaw and the way his pectoral muscles twitched, he stayed still, his expression like stone.

"I've never done this," I whispered, worried I couldn't pleasure him. And God, I wanted to so badly, just as much as he pleasured me.

"You know how fucking hot it is knowing I'll be your first?" He ran the crown of his cock over my lips, using it like a tube of lipstick, coating my flesh with his pre-cum. Painting me. "You know how possessive it makes me, knowing I'll be the only fucking man to ever see you like this?"

I might not have known what I was doing, but that didn't stop me from staring into his eyes and parting my lips to take his thick crown into my mouth. The muscles in his neck stood out, he gritted his teeth, and then he slid in slowly, inch by inch, until I was forced to brace my hands on his thighs to keep him from thrusting in too fast.

"Hollow out your cheeks," he gritted. "Move your tongue around." I was grateful for his direction. "Yeah... fuck yes. That's it... oh *Christ*, yes, Galina, that's it."

His encouragement fueled me on, and I moved my mouth over his cock, running my tongue along the flared tip, dipping it into the slit and lapping up the silky pre-cum that formed. I was starved for Arlo, it seemed, because I couldn't get enough. I was so lost on how good it made *me* feel to blow him that I didn't hear his low growl or how he told me to stop.

One second, I was sucking him off and enjoying the salty flavor of him, and the next, I was sitting bare-assed on the counter, my legs spread wide enough that Arlo could fit between them. He was still making those deep, growly noises, and I felt it all the way to my clit.

"When I come, it's going to be with my cock inside you and you taking every single last drop."

I looked down to watch him stroke himself, his dick wet-looking from my mouth, the tip having so much pre-cum that it started to drip onto the floor, a string of clear fluid hanging on to the crown before landing on the tile at his feet.

"If you aren't ready for this, you should tell me now."

I shook my head and braced my hands behind me on the counter, leaning back and thrusting my breasts out. I gave him that silent approval.

He hummed in pleasure and stepped closer to me, his body heat mixing with mine, the spicy, dark scent of him invading my senses. "I don't think I could have stopped anyway, *moy svet*." His tip was notched at my hole, his eyes locked on mine. I held my breath as he started pushing in, breaking through my virginity, tearing at my innocence, sliding deep inside me and stretching me until the pain and pleasure were so intense I felt a single tear slide down my cheek.

He leaned forward, one hand on the counter beside my ass, his other resting on my inner thigh to keep me spread. And when he flattened his tongue and licked up my cheek, taking that tear into him, I closed my eyes and moaned.

"Even your tears are the sweetest thing I've ever fucking tasted." He pushed in another inch. "Give me more. Let me lick them up, take a piece of you in me."

My head was thrown back, my hair hanging over the edge of the counter, and my eyes closed as I gave him what he asked for. The pain was front and center, the stretch so monumental I felt like I was splitting in two. But he was relentless as he pushed his way into me, burrowing himself into my body and into my heart inch by inch.

"Fuck yeah." He licked along my cheek again, getting every tear that slid from my eyes. And when he was fully inside me, we both exhaled harshly. "So tight. So fucking hot and tight for me. You're strangling my cock, baby."

I lifted my head and forced my eyes open. He rested his forehead against mine and started to pull out. I gasped right up against his mouth, and he kissed me, swallowing the sound, letting his cockhead stay notched right at my entrance before he pushed back in. We both shook from the force, groaning from the sensations.

"You deserve slow and easy for your first time—"

"I want *you* and how you want to be with me, Arlo." There was conviction in my voice as he pulled back, and we stared into each other's eyes. "I don't want some idea of how my first time is supposed to be." He was still for a second, only a twitch of his fingers on my hip before he growled and slammed back into me so hard my eyes widened and I cried out. He pulled out and looked down at his cock. I followed his gaze and saw his length covered in my arousal and streaked with my blood.

"Fuck," he seethed. "Look at how I broke you, took your innocence... made it fucking mine." He gripped my other hip and slammed home, my ass sliding up the counter, my skin squeaking along the surface. I could only hold on and watch as he fucked me with abandon, so fierce and untamed... exactly how I wanted it to be with him. The sounds of his cock tunneling into my pussy were so loud, my wetness making it dirty and obscene, but it had even more cream dripping from me, a slippery mess under my ass and making his thrusting so seamless all that discomfort morphed into a deliciously dark tendril.

"Look how good you take me, your little pussy sucking at my cock, tightening around me, milking me for my cum." His words were almost indiscernible, and with each one, I was soaring higher. "Touch yourself; play with your clit."

I slipped a shaky hand down my belly and ran my fingers along my bundle of nerves. I was wet, so drenched that when I lifted my fingers slightly, a string of wetness clung to the tip of my finger and connected with my pussy.

"Shit, that's hot."

I snapped my eyes up to his face and saw he watched where my hand was. I moved my fingers back to my clit and started rubbing it back and forth, a broken sound leaving me at the pleasure that coursed through me.

"Baby, I'm so fucking close already." His body was covered in sweat, glistening under the backdrop of city lights, his muscles flexing and relaxing as he pounded into me. "I'm going to come so fucking hard, and you're going to take every single drop I have to give you and ask for fucking more." He pulled my lower body closer to the edge of the counter and really started fucking me then.

"Yes." I worked my fingers over my clit while I let my head drop back on my neck and closed my eyes as I gave in to everything.

"Come for me."

And I did. I cried out long and loud, not caring who heard in the other apartments, not caring if I sounded like a wounded animal. I felt how hard my contractions were, how my pussy sucked and latched on to his cock. He was grunting and moving harder, his thrusting getting more erratic. I knew he was close, and when he slammed in deep and stilled, roaring out when he came, I felt his cock kick inside of me as he bathed every inch of me with his seed.

His cum was hot and thick and set off another orgasm that stole my breath and had my arms giving out under me. But before my back slammed onto the counter, Arlo's hand was pressed in the center of my back, his strong arm keeping me up.

Finally he stilled, resting his forehead on my chest, his warm breath washing along my breasts as we both panted and gasped for air. I lifted a hand and tunneled my fingers in his short hair, the strands damp at the temple. He kissed one of my breasts, then moved over and gave the other a gentle press of his lips. It seemed so intimate, maybe even more so than what we'd just shared.

I didn't know how long we stayed like that, with Arlo still semihard inside me, but my ass had since gone numb and I didn't care one bit. I'd never felt so alive and content before.

He lifted for me and pulled out, and instantly I felt our combined fluids start to come out of me on a warm trickle. Arlo was looking between my thighs, and I went to close them with embarrassment, knowing he could see his cum slipping from me, but he stilled me with his hands on my knees.

"No," he whispered gruffly and leaned in to press a kiss to my clit, pulling a sharp gasp from me. I felt his finger move along my entrance as he said, "How sore are you?"

I swallowed and took a few breaths before I answered. "Just a little."

"I bet." He kept gently rubbing along my entrance, gave my clit another kiss, and then I felt him push his cum back into my body. "I fucked you hard." I tried to stifle my moan, but it came out regardless. "I belong right in here." He lifted just his eyes to my face as he stayed between my thighs. "Always."

I found myself nodding before I could take in his words fully.

He stood, and I didn't fight him or complain when he lifted me into his embrace, my legs over his arm, my side to his chest, and my head on his shoulder. He held me gently, as if he cherished me. I closed my eyes and settled my weight against him, aching and sore between my thighs, the chill in the air and the experience we'd just shared causing goose bumps to skate along my arms and legs.

Arlo laid me on the bed and adjusted me so he could pull the blanket over my nude body. And then he was slipping in beside me and pulling me close, the warmth of his bare skin on mine pushing away all the coldness I'd felt and any worry or uncertainty that would have made itself known until there was only euphoria.

For long minutes we didn't speak, but I didn't know what we could have said. We spoke with our bodies and said so much during that time that I felt like I knew all I needed to about Arlo without him having to ever say a single syllable. I reached out for his hand that rested on his abdomen. I twined my fingers through his, staring at the contrast, how his hand was so much bigger than mine, his fingers so much longer.

His skin was a dark, golden hue compared to my pale complexion. He was strong where I'd always been weak. He was fearless where I'd always been afraid of what was lurking over my shoulder.

"I'm going after them, Galina," he said, his voice deep and wrapping around me like another blanket of protection.

I closed my eyes because I knew who he was talking about. He'd already killed Leonid, even if he hadn't said the words. I knew he was trying to protect me further. I'd never told him Henry's full name, never told him where he could be found, but I also knew if Arlo wanted to find someone, he didn't need me to accomplish that. He had resources I could never comprehend at his fingertips.

I thought about this man who held me so closely, who ran his fingers along my spine, always touching me, as if it centered him like it did me.

Arlo promised he'd make it safe for me, and that meant he was going to Vegas and after Henry. I knew without a doubt Arlo would kill him.

"I don't want any vengeance, Arlo." I rested my head on his chest and trailed my fingers over one of his many tattoos. I could see scars littering his flesh under that dark ink.

He stayed silent for long seconds before finally saying, "I'm going to make it safe for you, even if I have to kill everyone to make that reality." His arm around me tightened as if he needed to know I was still here.

"You don't have to ask for or need or want my vengeance, Galina. You have that from me without fail. You had it from the very beginning."

I should've been afraid of him, but I wasn't, and I knew I would never have cause to be. Talking him out of anything, especially something like this that caused the man who was clearly born out of blood and violence to latch on to like a starving beast, would have been like trying to break up two fighting dogs.

I'd only get hurt in the end, even if inadvertently.

22

Arlo

Sleep would never come tonight, not after killing Leonid, and not after claiming Galina. I'd held her for hours, her soft body molded to mine, the sweet scent that clung to her hair filling my nose every time I inhaled. Her arousal and virgin blood drying on my cock was a reminder that I didn't deserve her but that I wouldn't let her go.

I'd kept a constant touch on her, my fingers moving against her arm, down her back, brushing strands of silky dark hair away from her face just so I could look at her and watch her sleep.

I'd never considered myself a lucky man. That wasn't something life gave you. I'd scraped the bottom of the barrel to be able to survive, clawed my way out of a buried grave with dirt under my nails and blood covering my body just so I could make it the next day. But as I stared at Galina's sleeping face, counted each long, thick lash that formed dark crescents along her alabaster skin, I knew for the first time in my life, I *was* lucky. Because she was mine.

I'd been afraid of my turbulent emotions and the tightness in my body waking her, so for the last hour I'd been sitting at the table, cleaning my gun, the meticulous work good for my thoughts, helping calm the raging emotions inside me. They were foreign, not something I'd ever experienced or wanted, and they were all because of Galina. Now that I tasted them, I never wanted them to go away.

I could hear her stirring, imagined the sheets sliding against her smooth, bare skin. I was hard already, had been since she fell asleep in my arms, her head on my chest, her silky hair fanned across my chest.

My cock throbbed; my balls ached. I wanted her again. And again and again.

I felt my muscles tighten more as the need to fuck Galina again slammed into me. I wanted to tangle my hand in her hair and jerk her head back as I buried my face in the graceful line of her throat.

And as if my thoughts called her to me, she stepped out from the hallway, the white sheet wrapped around the lithe curves of her body. She had the material bunched together right above her breasts, one hand holding it in what I imagined was a white-knuckled grip.

The sight of her did something to my chest, something powerful and dangerous. Irreversible.

I set the piece I'd been cleaning down and pushed the chair back. Just enough. "Come here."

I saw the tightening of her nipples under that too-thin sheet as my words affected her. She didn't speak as she came forward, the material dragging softly against the hardwood, the *swoosh-swoosh* noise filling the thick silence.

She stopped a couple of feet from me, the pulse at the base of her ear telling me how her body responded to me. Fast. Erratic.

"Come closer, *malen'koye solnyshko.*" *Little sunshine.* That's what she was. Light to my darkness. Warmth to my cold.

Her eyes lowered to my cock, and she saw how hard I was for her already. *Come closer, Galina. Come closer to the wolf who's so hungry he'll devour you without a thought.*

And then she let the sheet fall away, her body

naked and soft, the lights from the city right outside the window whispering across her skin, the shadows playing along the perfect lines and curves of her form.

Come here and let me consume you like you've already done to me. Let me ruin you as much as you've caused every part of me to crumble to the gritty floor.

She took another step toward me, and another. I couldn't stop myself, didn't even try to act like I had any control where she was concerned. I reached out and curled my hand around her waist, my finger sticking into her soft flesh. Too hard, too forcefully. There would be marks tomorrow. But I couldn't find any reason to care. I wanted those bruises littering her soft, pale body. I wanted to be able to look at them and know she got them because of me... because she was mine.

I yanked her forward until she stumbled onto me, her legs on either side of my thighs. She straddled me, her pussy pressed right against my cock. She gasped, and I slid my hand up her waist, whispering along the curve of her breast before wrapping my fingers loosely around her throat. I added a little bit of pressure, a reminder that she was mine. A physical, visceral reminder to her. "Say it. Say the words."

She gasped, and I pulled her toward me even more, our lips barely brushing, her breath mixing with mine. I inhaled deeply, taking her into my lungs, needing to survive off her.

"Fuck me, Arlo."

I groaned and slammed my mouth down on hers, the beast coming alive once more and washing through me. I let go of her throat and gripped her waist, urging her to rise slightly. I grabbed the base of my cock, aligned the tip with her entrance, and then I was pulling her down, both hands on her hips, bruising fingers in her skin.

I tipped my head back and groaned loudly, the noise mixing with her gasp of pleasure and pain. I knew she was sore and told myself to be gentle. *Be easy.* But as she started riding me, I saw a haze of pleasure and need. I lifted my hips and pulled her down on me, fucked her like she was the air and I was suffocating.

I wanted to come in her again. I wanted to leave a little part of myself inside her like she'd done to me. Galina had worked her way into my body, torn away layer after layer, skinned me alive until I was the most vulnerable I'd ever been. And she didn't even know it. Would never grasp how naked I was.

"Mine," I growled right before I took her mouth

in a bruising kiss. She clutched at me as if she was afraid I'd ever let her go.

Never.

With Leonid gone, there was only one threat left to get rid of, and that was going to Vegas and finding the men Galina had run from, who'd threatened her, thought they could hurt and use her. I wouldn't wait. I'd do it right away, take Galina with me, because I couldn't stand to not have her by my side, my worry for her and the need to protect her too strong to ignore. She'd never be safer than when she was with me.

I was a strong man. An evil man. But for her, I wished I was good and gentle.

I wished I could be someone else entirely.

23

Galina

A handful of days had passed since Arlo claimed me, since I gave myself to a man for the first time.

Since he ruined me for all others and had put an invisible brand on me that deemed me as only his.

Even now I was still thinking about that first time... and the days that followed, how he'd taken me every night in his bed, in the shower, from behind, as I rode him. Being with Arlo was untamed, like we were two animals rutting together, sweaty and desperate, both needing to get off because it would be the final completion of bringing us together.

It had been wild and dirty. It had been aggressive and violent.

It was perfect.

And although all I wanted to do was stay wrapped in that fairy tale where the villain had made me his and I never had to worry about the what-ifs, reality was crashing back into me.

I stared out at the sight of Vegas. It had the same feel for me as it always did. Desperation, longing... hunger. It was a thick, sticky feeling that coated a person from head to toe, trying to suck them in with the flashing lights, the promise of euphoria and pleasure, the lie that if you just stayed a little bit longer, you'd fall in love.

A beautiful lie. For me at least.

But I knew there were the stupid in the world who embraced it all, if only for a moment in time. They'd get lost in how pretty things were on the outside, not knowing that if they dug a little deeper, they'd come to the rotten center. But I'd never been fooled, not when I spent my whole life nestled away in the slums where the beauty of what could be never touched you.

We'd taken a private jet from Desolation to Vegas almost two nights after Arlo killed Leonid. I wanted to tell him it was too soon, to let me think about this, for us to try to figure something else out. It wasn't that I was averse to him taking out Henry. In fact, when I thought about it, this sense of all things right filled me. And that scared me, terrified me that I was comfortable with the grit and destruction that came with the man I loved.

Because the truth was, I was sick in the head because I wanted Henry gone. I wanted my father to see the repercussions of what would happen if he tried to hurt me. I wanted Arlo to show everyone what he was capable of.

I didn't want to seem weak, never had been in my entire life, but for the first time ever, I felt as if I was cocooned in this bubble, as if I lived this whole other life. Feminists around the world would probably skin me alive at how much I loved the lengths Arlo would go to, to ensure my safety.

"It's time," Arlo said in his signature deep and gravelly voice from behind me.

I turned around but didn't move closer, feet upon feet separating us as he stood shrouded in shadows on the other end of the hotel room. He was magnificent and beautiful as I took in the suit he wore, a dark and expensive visage of what he really was.

A professional killer. A violent murderer with no remorse. A sociopath perhaps.

The man I love.

I made my way toward him until mere inches were the only thing keeping us apart.

"I'll say it again... I think it's best if you don't come so that you don't see what's going to happen."

I licked my lips and shook my head. He'd tried to tell me I wasn't going with him tonight—demanded I stay safely in the hotel room, more accurately. But if this was really going down, I *had* to be there. For my peace of mind and to close this chapter in my life.

"I'm coming," I said firmly—finally—and kicked up my chin in defiance, which had the corner of his mouth lifting in amusement despite the seriousness of the situation. He lifted his hand and cupped the side of my face. His expression softened.

"Grown men don't even have the balls to defy me." He leaned in and kissed me slowly and thoroughly, and I melted into him like I always did. "Your strength is one of the reasons I love you so fiercely." His words were low and deep and murmured against my mouth, and my pulse did a flip in my chest.

My heart pounded in my chest at his words. "I love you," I said, the words sounding like they'd been torn from me and rend me in half.

He pulled back, and I immediately rested my

forehead on the center of his chest, breathing in his scent. I loved this man so much it physically hurt, and although I knew nothing would happen to him because he was so strong and stubborn, so dangerous that even death feared him, my breath still hitched at the thought of losing him.

"There's no need for fear," he said softly and kissed the crown of my head. "Don't you know I'm the monster all other monsters fear?"

I smiled although I felt no humor in the way he teased, even if I knew he did it for my benefit.

"Come on. Let's get this over with."

I pulled back and looked up at him. I wanted the demons to stay firmly in the shadows. Yet I didn't want to ever look over my shoulder and worry someone would take me away from Arlo. And the only way to ensure our future was secure and our relationship stronger than ever was to have more bloodshed and bury the bodies of the past.

God, who was the woman I'd become, one who was okay with killing to ensure *my* life was safe?

A survivor. I'm a survivor, and I'll do anything to make sure I stay by Arlo's side.

After one more kiss, he led me out of the hotel room and down to the BMW that had been waiting for us at the airstrip once we landed. I didn't have to give Arlo any information about Henry or my father, and he'd never asked. Whatever connections he had, Arlo had obviously gotten the details he needed, and that was clear as we left the Strip and headed to Fremont Street.

The older part of Vegas came into view, a relic of the past yet still popular to tourists in the way they held on to a memento from a different time. But soon that facade started to wane the deeper we drove, the farther we went into the gritty part of what the city offered, where buildings were dilapidated, businesses run-down, broken windows and broken-down lives, with half-naked women standing on the corner of streets, smoking cigarettes and suggestively asking for "company tonight."

I felt myself get pulled back down to the only place I'd ever called "home," and I hated it. I felt nauseous in the way it was heavy inside me, like this other presence trying to take root in my soul.

I was staring out the passenger window when I felt Arlo's hand cover mine that rested on my thigh. I looked over at him, but he was firmly focused on the street ahead. I wasn't surprised he'd been able to sense my turbulent emotions. We were connected in a way I'd never understand but was forever grateful for.

He tightened his fingers on my hand, and I lifted my other to place my palm over his, the warmth and strength that poured from Arlo enough to have a semblance of calm washing over me. But even that soothing sensation couldn't fully extinguish my bone-deep fear of what was happening next.

The broken part of Vegas was like another world on its own with how things worked. It was like Desolation in that sense, with life lost in the deepest parts, swallowed whole and decaying in the underbelly of what used to be a thriving society.

I didn't know how long we drove, but it was done in silence. I looked over at Arlo again, seeing and sensing the change in him the closer we got to wherever our destination was. His body was tighter, his concentration sharper. He had retreated to some hidden part of himself where emotions couldn't touch, where he was a machine without feeling and only had cold, dead calculation as his compass. I focused out the windshield again, because if I thought about this too hard, I'd have to retreat into myself to get through this.

It was another five minutes before Arlo finally slowed and pulled the BMW into the cracked and uneven parking lot where an old casino sat. It didn't even look like it was still operating for business, but there was a flickering light above the scarred and faded front door, like a welcome mat for anyone brave—or stupid—enough to enter.

He maneuvered the car toward the back of the building where no light touched before turning around so he faced the street. He cut the engine, and we sat in silence for long seconds as he stared at the back of the casino, both of us plunged into darkness so shapes were distorted and reality didn't quite look how it should.

"Arlo?" I whispered his name but didn't know what I was asking him.

"You'll stay in the car, Galina." He looked at me then, the first time since we'd left the hotel. He reached over and opened the glove box, a dim light from the small interior breaking up the density of the blackness. He pulled out a gun and held it to me, the barrel facing the windshield. I glanced from the weapon back to him. His silence was loud, his message clear.

Use this if anyone fucks with you.

I reached out and took the gun, our fingers brushing together for a split second before the contact was broken. The weight of the weapon was substantial as I stared down at it, the metal cold but warming the longer I held it. I knew how to shoot, had to learn at a young age. But this weapon was heavy in my palm, bigger than the one I owned, and I felt a light sheen of perspiration cover my forehead.

"Arlo, let's just go," I suddenly said and snapped my focus to his face. "I just want you to be safe. Let's go and forget this." I was rambling, my fear so strong right now I couldn't control myself. And I felt ashamed over that. *Right now I need to be strong.* I'd never let fear control me, but at the thought of Arlo getting hurt—or worse—this cold terror encompassed me.

"*Moy svet*," he murmured. "You have nothing to be afraid of. I won't let anyone hurt you." His jaw tightened. "I won't let anyone take you from me."

I shook my head because he'd misunderstood me. "I don't care about me. I can't lose *you*," I said and was immediately embarrassed. I didn't want to cling to what we had, to let it be a weakness, but here I was, begging him to leave with me so there wasn't a threat that he'd be taken from me.

"My sweet Galina," he whispered and cupped my face as he leaned in and kissed my lips softly, then the tip of my nose, and finally settled on my forehead. I closed my eyes and let the feeling and smell of him surround me until that hard panic started to lessen.

"Not even death can take me from your side." He pulled back and looked me in the eyes. "Not even death," he said again, and I nodded, although I wanted to tell him he couldn't guarantee that. No one was immortal or invincible. No one could predict when or how they died, or stop it. But when Arlo said it with such stony determination and finality in his voice, it was hard *not* to believe that if anyone could defy death itself, it was him.

"Tell me you understand." His voice was hard, as if he expected me to comply no matter what, to believe my words even if they were a lie.

It was hard to breathe, let alone speak, but I managed to say, "Okay. I understand that you're crazy." I was the one to lean in and kiss him this time and felt his lips tilt into a smile against mine.

"*U nas yest' vsya nasha zhizn', chtoby byt' pravymi.*" He pulled back and smoothed a finger over my bottom lip. "We have our entire lives to be together." And then he was out of the car, the locks engaging, sealing me in, the gun in my hand a reminder that I had to use it. Because although I told him I'd stay in the car, there was no way I was letting him go into that situation alone. There was no way I'd let him get hurt because he was making things safe for me.

With steely reserve, I'd do what I had to, like I'd always done.

I'd fight for my life, and Arlo was now firmly embedded in it.

I'd fight to the death for both of us if need be.

24

Galina

The night seemed colder than it should for this time of year, or maybe it was the worst fear I'd ever felt in my life taking hold.

I'd been standing outside the back door of this broken casino for a long moment, my back against the brick, my breathing so fast and erratic I feared someone passing by would hear.

The sound of music blaring in the distance, the screeching laughter of a woman far too close for comfort, the crash of glass breaking, and an array of other obnoxious noises filtered through the night and tried to pull my concentration in twenty different directions.

The man you love is in there fighting for you. Go in there and stand by his side.

He'd hate it, be pissed at me. But I didn't care. Not right now, not when doing nothing wasn't an option.

With one more steadying breath, I pushed away from the wall, drawing up all the calm concentration I could muster, and reached for the back door I'd seen Arlo step through.

I curled my hand around the handle and pulled it open, the metal giving a loud creak, which had me freezing and my breath stalling in my lungs, my heart in my throat as I prayed to whoever was willing to listen that no one heard. After a second where no one came rushing toward me with their gun raised, I stepped inside.

I shut the door as quietly as I could behind me, the scent of mold and age tickling my nose in an uncomfortable way. The back room I stepped into had boxes pushed against the walls on either side of me. Trash littered the floor, grime and dirt everywhere. The ceiling looked like it was ready to cave in, bowing in one corner, the rest of the once-white paneling showing water damage that created large brown and yellow circles above my head.

I could hear muffled voices coming through the

closed door in front of me, and I quietly made my way toward it, gripped the handle, and pulled it open. I immediately scented cigar smoke, but it couldn't mask the stench of heavy mold and decay thick in the air.

When I stepped out into the small hallway, I followed the muted light that came from my left, which was also where the voices filtered from. I was surprised I wasn't shaking, my hands steady, my finger running slowly over the gun as if a reminder of what I'd have to do. Because there was no doubt in my mind I'd have to use it on somebody to protect myself and Arlo.

I stopped before I got to the edge of the hallway that opened into the main part of the building, and looked around the side, taking in the large room that had clearly once been the main casino. Broken-down and half-taken-apart slot machines were pushed up against walls.

I could see a blackjack table with torn and stained felt laying on its side on the ground and to the left. There was one window beside the front doors, the glass painted black, a piece of cardboard taped in the corner, presumably to cover up a hole.

And then my heart jumped into my throat when

I spotted where the men were, where the voices came from, and how Arlo stood behind Henry with a gun pointed at the back of his head. There were only two other men seated at the card table, one on each side of Henry, both looking ready to shit themselves.

Arlo had his other hand up, another gun pointed at one of the men.

"Go ahead," Arlo said calmly as he looked at the man who sat to his right, the only one who didn't have a gun pointed to a skull. "Reach for it, grab your weapon, and we'll see how fast you are." Arlo slowly grinned, and it was a smile I'd never seen before. It was absolutely terrifying. "You're all gambling men here. Want to place a wager that I can put a bullet in all three of your skulls before you even draw?"

A thick moment of silence passed where no one spoke. I don't even think they breathed.

The man sat stiffly in his chair as he stared at Arlo. There was no doubt in my mind, given his expression, that he wouldn't be taking on that bet.

"You're making a big mistake," Henry had the balls to say.

Arlo chuckled softly, but there was nothing humorous about it. It was dark and insidious, as if it was a precursor to all the "mistakes" that would come. "Is that so? You're some big shot, huh?"

Henry narrowed his eyes despite Arlo not looking at him.

"It's usually men who are about to die who say it's a mistake," Arlo said in a deceptively calm voice. I could hear the sound of trickling, something wet hitting the ground. My vantage point allowed me to see one of the men had pissed his pants, urine trailing down his leg and creating a puddle on the floor.

"You fucking weak asshole," Henry sneered as he clearly realized one of his spiders had lost his bladder. Arlo pressed the gun harder against Henry's skull, and he straightened in his seat, gritting his teeth. "You have no idea who you're messing with."

No, Henry had no idea who *he* was messing with.

"You stupid girl." The low voice that came from behind me and the feel of a gun pressing into the center of my back had my entire body freezing. But it wasn't the gun pressed between my shoulder blades that had me tightening. It was the voice... the voice of my father. "You should have stayed away. Not like Henry wasn't gonna find you." His breath was warm and thick with the scent of booze. "He did find you, was gonna bring you back. You've made my life hell by skipping out."

I looked over my shoulder at my father. His face was beat to hell, black-and-blue and swollen. It was clear me leaving had caused Henry to use the man who'd been my sperm donor as his personal punching bag. Yet I felt nothing. No sympathy. No empathy.

He nudged my back with the gun until I stumbled forward. Arlo lifted his eyes in my direction, but other than a subtle tic in his jaw, he showed no emotion. He might keep that steely composure, but I knew he was pissed I was here, that I hadn't listened. Surely he knew I couldn't allow him to do this on his own. He had to know I'd stand beside him to make this right.

This was my fight, and I wouldn't do it in the safety of a car with a gun in my lap as someone else put their life on the line for me.

Henry started laughing, and not even the gun pressed to his head could stop him. "So this is your doing, Galina?"

A low rumble filled the room, and I realized it came from Arlo. He leaned in so his lips were close to Henry's ear and said something in a voice too low to carry to me. I could see Henry's skin become pale, his eyes flashing with fear, but then they shifted to something evil as he stared at me.

When Arlo stood, his eyes were trained on my father, who stood behind me. He now had a firm grip on my arm as if he thought I'd try to run. But I was done running. I was sick of hiding. I was here to face this head-on no matter the consequences.

When we stood a foot from the card table and off to the side, the two other men sitting glanced my way with terror clear on their faces. They were lackeys, pawns in whatever sick game Henry played.

"Henry, just give them what they want. He's not playing."

Henry looked to the side and bared his teeth at the man who'd spoken. "Fucking coward." He wasn't smart, not even with a gun pressed to his head. He kept his fear covered in knock-off designer suits and too much cheap cologne.

The gun was ripped out of my hand by my father, but he still had his gun pressed to my back. But as I stared into Arlo's face, I wasn't afraid of dying. At that moment I wasn't afraid of anything. My entire life and all the situations I'd experienced so far had come full circle. I knew from this moment on that I would never allow anything to control me. I wouldn't allow someone to scare me enough to have me running away. It always caught up with you anyway.

Henry looked me up and down, his gaze lewd and just as slimy as I remembered. He grinned and spat out, "Lookin' just as perfect as the last time I saw you, Galina. I wonder if that tight little virgin cunt is still untouched, or if you became the whore I envisioned shaping you into myself."

Pop.

I blinked once, my ears ringing, that *bang* of a gun being discharged echoing throughout the entire room, seeming to shake the lone window and crack it even more. I stared at where Henry sat, the bullet hole in his head leaving a trail of red right between his eyes and down the bridge of his nose.

He slumped forward, his skull cracking against the card table hard enough the flimsy piece of furniture shook from the force.

"Holy shit."

"Fuck!" the two men on either side of him screamed out, eyes wide, their fear saturating the room.

"Man, we had nothing to do with whatever Henry was into," one guy rambled, hands in front of him.

"We just help him occasionally," the other man cried.

"Oh holy fuck. Please don't kill us."

Arlo looked right at me, and without taking his gaze off mine, he pointed one gun at the guy to the right and kept the other one trained on the man to the left. Then he pulled the triggers and shot them both perfectly in the head. It all happened in a matter of seconds, yet also seemed to go so slow it was like wading through water.

Three bodies now slumped over the card table, blood seeping into the green felt, my father behind me cursing, the gun at my back shaking from his nerves.

The scent of blood filling the room became so strong my stomach twisted, bringing me back to the present, time speeding up until I could remember to breathe again.

"Let her go," Arlo said and aimed the gun right over my shoulder. He was a good shot, but how good of one when I was being used as a shield?

"Put the gun down and let me go. I ain't got no fight in this," my coward father mumbled from behind me. It was because of *him* that all of this was even happening.

My father had his arm raised and pointed the

gun at Arlo as he started slowly backing up, one arm around my chest as he kept me firmly in place so if anyone got shot, it was me. "I mean it. Let me go or she dies."

"You'd shoot your daughter to save your own ass?" Arlo asked calmly as he moved away from the table and came forward, staying far enough back that my father wasn't spooked any more than he already was.

"She's nothing to me."

And wasn't that the truth. Nothing but a bargaining tool. Nothing but someone to sell to be raped and tortured just so his debts could be paid. I'd never meant anything to him, and that's why when he rounded the corner with me, I pulled up the self-defense moves Arlo had taught me and leaned into him. It took him off guard at first, his hold loosening marginally, and it gave me enough leverage to twist in his hold, turn sharply, and bring my knee up to connect with his groin.

He grunted and brought his arm up. I knew he was about to shoot and saw it happening in slow motion. I ducked and put all my weight into his body, careening us to the wall. His back slammed into it, the air leaving him, my head ringing as his skull cracked into mine from the impact. I knew the only reason I'd caught him off guard was because he was drunk and he'd underestimated me.

We wrestled with the gun for only a second, the weapon between us, our eyes locked on each other's. I saw his desperation, knew he'd kill me if it meant saving his own hide. If I had any sentimental value toward this man, it would have been crushed a long time ago. As it was, all I saw was my survival or him bringing me down to hell with him.

The gun exploded between us, going off, heat, smoke, and searing pain encompassing me in a physical and emotional way. We both froze, staring wide-eyed at the other, both hands on the weapon. I stumbled back and looked down, the barrel pointed at my father's chest. Blood seeped through his shirt and spread outward so fast I took another step back. I slammed into a hard wall—Arlo's chest. He gently took the gun from me, wrapped a protective arm around my waist, and then lifted his arm.

My father was shaking his head and holding his hands out, pleading, begging as he bled out, but it all fell on deaf ears and apathy. Arlo fired his gun and delivered a bullet right through one of his eyes. My father's head cracked back on the wall before he slid down to the ground, blood smearing as he made his descent.

I didn't know how long I stood there, but when Arlo wrapped me in his arms, my head over his heart, the tears came fast and strong. They weren't ones of sadness or fear. They were ones of pure, utter relief.

I was finally free, even if I was covered in blood.

25

Galina

They were both dead, that chapter in my life done. No more running. No more hiding.

It was enough to have a tear unexpectedly slide down my cheek.

I wrapped my arms around my waist and stared out at the bright lights of Vegas. The sights and sounds, the bustle of life that had always been a constant in my world seemed miles away. A distant memory.

It was no longer my past or present. Because my future was so very different now.

"No more tears."

I closed my eyes at the sound of Arlo and felt

another tear move down my cheek as if my body was trying to defy his very words.

"It's over," I whispered and opened my eyes at the same time I turned around to face him. He immediately enveloped me in his arms and held me, resting his chin on the crown of my head, my strong protector who asked for nothing in return but gave me so much of himself.

"I love you." I uttered the words, not realizing they'd come out until I felt his body tense against mine. "I love you so much," I sobbed, meaning them with every single part of me.

He tangled his hand in my hair, the locks damp from the shower we'd taken together as soon as we'd gotten back to the hotel hours ago. He'd washed me so gently, wiping away the violence of the night, as if he needed to do it so desperately it was his only mission in life.

He tipped my head back so I was forced to look into his face, the light from the city coupled with the darkness of the room casting an ominous presence over him. I stared into his eyes and got lost in the depths. "I love you," I whispered, wanting to say the words over and over again until they were seared on our flesh, forever tattooed on our souls.

I lifted my hands and cupped his cheeks, a light

scruff starting to grow in, scratching along the sensitive skin of my palms.

He was brutally beautiful, my dark, avenging angel. He made me feel things that I'd never thought possible, that I'd never envisioned for myself. I never thought I could give my heart to somebody, that I'd ever truly feel safe or be happy.

But looking into the dark, turbulent emotions that covered Arlo's face, I knew without a doubt all the things that had led up to this point in my life, all the ugly things had brought me to this one beautiful moment in time.

They led me to him.

"*Moy svet.* I love you as much as my dead, dark, and twisted heart can love anything so light and beautiful. I'll love you until I can't love anymore, and only then it'll be because I'm dead and rotting in the ground."

I rose up on my toes and pressed my lips to his, stopping him from saying anything. I dragged my tongue across the seam of his mouth, loving the spicy, masculine flavor that covered him—that *was him*—before delving inside. He was still so tense, but he tightened his fingers in my hair, holding me in place as he tilted my head to the side and deepened things.

This harsh groan left his throat, and I couldn't help but soften against him, wanting that danger and darkness that seeped from his soul and surrounded me. "I need you," I begged against his mouth, not realizing until this moment that I'd never needed anything more than I needed to feel Arlo's body pressed against mine, his cock deep in my pussy, his power holding me down so I was forced to take it all.

The feeling of his arms tightening around me had a thrill moving through my entire core. I found myself tearing at his clothes, ripping at mine, needing to be bare, to feel skin on skin, to know Arlo wanted me as much as I wanted him. I needed to know I was alive at this moment.

And when the remains of our clothing were nothing but tatters on the ground, he lifted me up, his biceps clenching with power. I wrapped my legs around his waist, my arms around his neck, deepening the kiss, desperate and hungry, starved like an animal unleashed inside us.

"I need to fuck you," he growled against my mouth and didn't wait for me to comply, to agree... to beg to be filled and stretched by him.

He strode us toward the bedroom, and I repeated, "I need you." Arlo kissed me and growled between licks and sucks, his hands gripping my ass cheeks, his palms so big and firm, so masculine. The air left me when my back hit the mattress, when Arlo's massive frame covered mine.

He used his knees to spread my legs wide, pushing them out forcefully so I had no choice but to stretch for him, to bare my pussy and wait for him to give it to me the way I wanted. And when he settled fully on top of me, the thick, heavy length of his cock sliding right between my pussy lips, I tunneled my hands in his hair and tugged on the strands as a moan was ripped from me.

"So fucking wet for me." He thrust against me, his length slipping up and down my slit before moving back. Over and over, he slid through my cunt, my lips framed around his girth, the root of his shaft rubbing my clit with every upstroke.

"Arlo. God, yes." I could have gotten off on this alone, the rocking motion, the feel of his weight on me, pushing me down on the bed, making me take what he had to give me.

I was so wet, soaked, my inner thighs smeared with my arousal for him.

"So ready for me," he growled against the side of my neck, biting down on the flesh hard enough I cried out from pleasure and pain, knowing there would be bruises come morning, fingertip-sized ones on my waist, hickeys on my neck.

I speared my hands in his hair, keeping him right where he was, begging for more, harder... all of it. I lifted my hips, silently demanding. I needed him inside me so deep I didn't know where I ended and he began.

And then the tip nudged at my pussy hole a second before he lifted his head slightly and looked me in the eyes. "*Moya.*" *Mine.* He thrust all those inches into me so hard my back arched, my breasts shook, and a painfully aroused sound left my mouth. "You're mine," he grunted as he thrust into me hard once more, sliding out until the tip was lodged in my entrance, then pushed back in.

"Yes," I cried out.

He fucked me with fast strokes, ones that made me feel like he was staking his claim irrevocably, that he was showing me with his body that I'd never get away, that I was his. His hips slammed against me, the sloppy, wet sound of our fucking so dirty, so raunchy, that I was almost on the verge of coming from that alone.

He was brutal, the motions pushing me up the bed from the force. Arlo slipped his hand under me and up my back, curling his fingers over one shoulder, keeping me in place as he worked his cock in and out of me.

This wasn't making love. This was raw, hard-core fucking. He was a feral beast, his body corded with strength and deadly precision. It was like he was losing just as much control as I felt like I was inside. And all I could do was hold on to him, my legs wrapped around his waist, my hands still tangled in his hair. He was biting and licking at my neck, making inhuman sounds that drove me perilously close to orgasm. His grunts, my moans, and the noise of our wet sex slapping together surrounded my head and filled the room.

"You're mine, and I will never let you go." He slammed so hard into me, hitting a secret spot that had my eyes rolling back in my head and the air being forced from my lungs. "Now come for me."

I came, my body obeying Arlo instantaneously.

"Fuck yeah. That's it. Even your body knows you're mine."

The vibrations from his voice went right to my clit, engorging the tiny bundle even more until I was nothing but a mindless fiend, thrashing my head back and forth, trying to stay conscious. I knew Arlo was the only thing that could give me the fix I needed. He was the only thing that had brought life into every single part of me.

He grabbed both of my wrists in one of his hands and thrust my arms above my head, adding pressure and pinning me down so I was spread out like an offering. And then Arlo leaned back, his other hand gripping my waist, his fingers clenching and relaxing as he stared down at where our bodies were connected.

"I've never seen anything hotter than the sight of my cock in your cunt." He slid in and pulled back out, slow and easy, as if he savored the sight. "My cock is so wet, glossy because you're fucking dripping for me." His gaze refused to move from where he watched, and I lifted my head to look down the length of my body to watch too. My lips parted as I saw the thick, girthy length of his shaft pull out of my body, wet and shiny under the glow of the outside lights coming through the window.

"Look how wet you are, baby. Look at how fucking soaked you've made my cock."

"Yes, Arlo. Oh God, yes. Fuck me."

And he did just that.

He slid his hands along my inner thighs, then hooked his fingers under my knees, pushing my legs out so far and wide that my muscles protested in the best way. The new position was obscene, my legs damn near in the splits position, my pussy lewdly displayed, but God, I'd never found anything hotter.

He slammed into me so hard and fast that I was losing my mind.

Arlo was ruthless, my body aching wonderfully. My breasts shook back and forth, my nipples hard peaks, painful, silently begging for his mouth again. As if he knew my thoughts, knew what I *needed*, he bent down and took one taut tip into his mouth, drawing the bud up, running his teeth gently over it again and again until my pussy clenched tightly around his cock on its own with my impending orgasm.

"So sweet. My favorite flavor in the world is *you*." He dragged his tongue over my chest, up my neck, and circled my ear before growling out, "Now come for me."

And I did. I exploded in a show of lights and fireworks, pain and pleasure. All I could do was take what he gave me. Every single touch, sight, smell, and sound drove me higher.

The gruff sounds he made against my throat as he thrust in and out of me. The way his balls slapped the crease of my ass. How the root of his shaft rubbed against my clit every time he slammed home.

I was flying high, licking the sky, feeling that ecstasy from the tips of my toes to the ends of my hair. And I never wanted it to end.

I felt his cock kick inside me, growing thicker before he roared out, the heavy, hot jets of his cum filling me, taking root so I'd always be marked from the inside out by the man who held my heart, body, and soul.

When we were both spent and depleted, he brought one of my hands to his mouth, kissed the center of my palm, and then braced his forearms on the bed on either side of my head. Our breathing was harsh and identical, our skin sweaty. I felt the droplets of his perspiration land on my chest, hot and sticky... so damn sexy.

He pulled out, and I felt the loss right away. I felt the combination of my arousal and his cum slip from my pussy and slide down the crease of my ass to make a wet spot on the mattress.

Arlo pulled me close to him, and I curled against his body, my head dizzy, my vision blurry from the aftereffects of my orgasm, of my sheer happiness and love for this man. He lifted my hand and placed it on his chest, right over his heart. I tipped my head back to look into his face, noticing he already watched me, *knowing* there was something on his mind. There was a strange expression on his face, one I couldn't place. I reached up and smoothed my finger between the crease of his eyes.

"I never had a heart to give away, Galina," he said softly in the darkness, his gaze holding mine. "I never knew love, never gave it or received it. I didn't even know what it was until you came along."

My heart stalled in my chest at hearing him say those words, my breath holding in my lungs as I waited for him to continue.

"I'm not a good man. You know this. And you accept me regardless." He took my hand and placed it on his chest, right over his heart. "But whatever can grow in this dark, dead heart of mine, whatever love I am capable of, I want you to own it. I want you to be the only person to have that part of me, *moy svet*."

"Arlo—"

"I want to give you everything that I am, Galina. I want to give you the bad, the good... even the parts that are terrifying, because that's what's real; that's who I am." He slid his hand along the side of my neck to cup my face, his thumb smoothing over my temple. "I didn't know what being in love felt like, and until you came along, I never knew how much I wanted to live. For you."

"I love you." I said those three words again, tears building in my eyes, ones that came from the very best part of me.

"Without you, there is no me, Galina. And if that's love, then I love you so fucking much I'd tear my heart out and give it to you in offering just so you could see my loyalty, my determination... that within this monster, I am just a man needing the most important person in his life. *You*."

I closed my eyes and felt a smile move across my face.

"I love you. So much you make life hurt in the very best way, *moy svet*."

And that's how I fell asleep, knowing I'd never have to be afraid of what lived in the dark any longer, because I had the most dangerous monster holding me tight.

EPILOGUE

Arlo

Five years later

You can never fully leave behind darkness. It follows you like a shadow, always there, looking and imposing. But as long as you have light, it will always stay one step behind, never able to touch you.

And as long as I had Galina in my life, I'd never truly be the villain in my own story. She'd given me that humanity I'd always been missing.

I stood on the porch and stared at her, her profile shadowed by the sun setting over the horizon, the waves crashing against the shore. Next to staring into

Galina's face, the sight of her like this, the beach and ocean her backdrop, was one of the most beautiful things I'd ever seen.

For three years we'd lived on the shores of a small French village, the beach butting right up against our home, the salt and seawater in the air. I knew leaving the Ruin behind had been the best decision I could have ever made. Because it made Galina happy.

I'd waited to get my affairs and finances in order and had been putting all the money I earned working for the Ruin into offshore accounts so that no one—legitimate or otherwise—could ever get their hands on it. I had to ensure we'd never be followed, her life never again put in the crosshairs. I'd hated waiting so long to get her out of that godforsaken city and life, but it had been worth it. To see her smile up at me every night when I made love to her told me that without any words being uttered.

To know I'd done everything in my power to ensure Galina would never have to want for anything again in her life gave me peace. And I'd been ensuring that since I started working with the Ruin. But my priorities had shifted over the last five years—ever since Galina came into my life. Now, the end goal and all the saving had been to make her happy and keep her safe.

Until I took my last breath, I'd always make sure she was provided for, looked after, taken care of. I loved her. So fucking much.

I walked toward my wife, who stood in the same spot where we'd taken our vows nearly three years before. Galina had her arms hanging loosely at her sides, the wind moving her long Bohemian-style skirt back and forth.

I stepped up behind her and wrapped my arms around her slightly swollen belly, my palms flat on the swell as I leaned down and nuzzled her neck. She tilted her head to the side to give me better access, and I closed my eyes and inhaled her sweet scent.

"What are you thinking about, *moy svet*?"

She wrapped her arms around mine, and I could practically *feel* her smile. "You and how happy you make me."

I kissed the side of her neck again. I wasn't a good man. I never had been, and I never would be. Galina was the only saving grace in my life, my soft spot, my weakness. She knew all of this, listened to me tell her my darkest parts, my past, the violent

things I'd done. And she loved me regardless, irrevocably. Undeniably.

*"Ya nikogda ne znal, chto znachit byt' zhivym,
prezhde chem ty byl moim."*

She turned and wrapped her arms around my
neck, rising on her toes to bring her lips flush with
mine. "I understood you pretty well that time," she
murmured against my lips.

"Yeah?" I nibbled her bottom lip. She'd started
learning Russian and French a few years back, the
latter something practical since we now called France
home, the former because she said she had a passion
for learning how she could curse me out when I
pissed her off. I'd grinned, not caring if she wanted to
swear at me in Russian every day. Her voice was so
lovely anything she said was music to my ears.

"That's right," she kept teasing. She pulled back,
and her expression turned somber. "I never knew
what it meant to be alive before you were mine."

She said the exact phrase I'd just told her in
Russian, and although I told her she was mine, I
knew she'd never understand when I told her she
was the only thing that had ever made me feel alive.

"I love you," I whispered and kissed her slowly. I
slipped my fingers over her belly again just as my

little girl, growing safely inside her mother, kicked my hand strongly.

"I hope you're ready for her, because I'm afraid how active she is while inside is a precursor to how wild she'll be once she's here."

I kissed her again and again, unable to stop my grin. "I can't fucking wait. Let her be a wild child. Let her experience life and the world as she wants. No one will hold her back, or I'll put a bullet in their head."

Galina snorted and rolled her eyes, but I was fucking serious. My baby girl wouldn't be told she couldn't ever accomplish anything in this world. I'd never be like my father. I'd teach her about the world, the good and bad and how she could overcome any obstacle. And I'd do that with the one person I trusted more than anything else: my wife, soul mate, mother of my children—because I wanted a houseful of daughters who looked just like Galina and sons who would protect the women in their lives above all else.

She was my heart. My light.

I was lucky to have Galina in my life, luckier still that I was going to be a father. I'd never complain about anything again, not when I'd been given the best gift imaginable.

Happiness, love, and—most of all—knowing what it meant to actually live.

Want to read more in the Underworld Kings series? Check out **RECKLESS HEIR**, Nikolai's story, coming February 2022!

ABOUT THE AUTHOR

Find Jenika at:

www.JenikaSnow.com

Jenika_Snow@yahoo.com

Printed in Great Britain
by Amazon